the

DEFINITION

of

BEAUTIFUL

THE
DEFINITION
OF
BEAUTIFUL

a memoir

CHARLOTTE
BELLOWS

Freehand Books acknowledges the financial support for its publishing program provided by the Canada Council for the Arts and the Alberta Media Fund, and by the Government of Canada through the Canada Book Fund.

 Canada Council Conseil des Arts Alberta ∎ Canadä
for the Arts du Canada   Government

Freehand Books
515–815 1st Street SW   Calgary, Alberta   T2P 1N3
www.freehand-books.com

Book orders: UTP Distribution
5201 Dufferin Street   Toronto, Ontario   M3H 5T8
Telephone: 1-800-565-9523   Fax: 1-800-221-9985
utpbooks@utpress.utoronto.ca   utpdistribution.com

Library and Archives Canada Cataloguing in Publication
Title: The definition of beautiful : a memoir / Charlotte Bellows.
Names: Bellows, Charlotte, author.
Identifiers: Canadiana (print) 20230461107 | Canadiana (ebook) 20230461123 | ISBN 9781990601460 (softcover) | ISBN 9781990601477 (EPUB) | ISBN 9781990601484 (PDF)
Subjects: LCSH: Bellows, Charlotte. | LCSH: Bellows, Charlotte—Health. | LCSH: Bellows, Charlotte—Mental health. | LCSH: Anorexia nervosa—Patients—Canada—Biography. | LCSH: Eating disorders in women. | LCSH: Body image in women. | LCSH: Body image in girls. | LCGFT: Autobiographies.
Classification: LCC RC552.A5 B45 2023 | DDC 616.85/2620092—DC23

Dictionary definitions from Google's English dictionary, provided by Oxford languages.

Edited by Naomi K. Lewis
Book design by Natalie Olsen
Cover image © Natasa Kukic / Stocksy.com
Author photo by Trudie Lee
Printed on FSC® recycled paper and bound in Canada by Friesens

A *note to the reader*

This book includes descriptions of the physical effects of starvation. If you find yourself comparing and wanting to attain such a weight, please shut the book and reach out for help. I share with you my story not for comparison, but to help you and others throw aside harmful beliefs and seek a full, healthy body like you and I were meant to live in.

en·tro·py

/ˈentrəpē/

noun

1. lack of order or predictability;
   gradual decline into disorder.

ROCK BOTTOM

I didn't hear the words the doctor said.

But I remember the way the room wilted beneath his somber tone.

When I look back to that evening, hundreds of little details come rushing into my memory, but not a single one of those details is a word. Some things are simply too powerful to be spoken, I guess. The only way to know it exists is to feel it.

The hospital room was cold. I was always cold now, but I felt especially cold at that moment. The entire room some strange, alien place.

I didn't like it because I didn't belong there.

Or maybe I didn't like it because I did.

It was just like every other hospital room I'd ever seen: cramped for space, sterile white, an apparatus of complicated-looking machines set up beside a stiff bed. Technically, there was nothing different or special about it. It felt different, though. Something about this hospital room was vast and lonely; it made me feel inexplicably small.

I could hear the doctor talking with my mom outside the closed hospital door. I wasn't supposed to hear any of what they said — that's why they had left me in this room. Still, I've learned that hospital walls are remarkably not soundproof at all. Knowing this, I'm sure, the doctor spoke in a low, murmuring tone.

I glanced over at the machines beside the bed. The only reason I was here was because of little numbers that came up on the screens when I was hooked up to those machines. All of this, because of *numbers*.

One of them had a blue cuff with a cord attached to it. Blood pressure.

The other had a tangle of cords that had been attached to various points of my torso with cold stickers. I'd already pulled them off, but they'd left patches of sticky residue on the left side of my chest. To see how strong my heart was, I assumed.

Outside the room and down the hall stood a scale. The one machine that really mattered. They'd made me turn around and step onto it backwards, so I couldn't see the number that came up. I guess that made sense. Still, I'd tried to subtly twist my head and look out of the corner of my eye. Unfortunately, the nurse noticed this and quickly covered the number from my view with a piece of paper. She asked me to step off.

After that, they led me to this room.

As I sat on the hard hospital bed and waited, my mind was consumed with thoughts of what that number might have been. I tried to factor in everything I'd eaten the past week. It didn't take long until I'd lost track of all the numbers in my head; I sighed.

From outside, the doctor droned on. Time had never passed so slowly. I just wanted my mom to step back into the room and drive me home.

The doctor's voice stopped.

Silence.

A long, still silence.

Then, that silence was broken by the quiet sniffling of my mom. It was a fragile cry. I could tell by the little gasping sounds she made that she was trying to keep it in.

I pulled my knees towards my chest and wrapped my arms around my shins.

The doctor had done it — he'd delivered the news. I already knew it; in fact, I'd known it for many months. Out of all the things I felt, surprise was not one of them.

I rested my forehead against my knees and closed my eyes. My knees felt bony and uncomfortable as they pressed up against my head, but I didn't mind. I tried to focus on any sensation other than hearing.

Several seconds later, the crying stopped. Finally, the door creaked open, and I looked up.

Mom's eyes, peering out from behind her mask, were slightly red and blotchy.

"Ready to go home, sweetie?" she asked with a strained voice, trying to sound cheery.

I nodded.

The doctor printed out a small stack of papers and handed them to my mom, which she immediately folded and stuffed into her large purse. She followed me out, and we walked through the empty hospital halls. We passed by the scale, and I had an urge to jump on it and see what number came up. I knew Mom had already had an awful time, even more awful than me, possibly. I didn't want to make it any worse.

Plus, I just really wanted to get out.

Our footsteps echoed slightly as we walked down the too-shiny floor and towards the exit.

It was a dry, blustery day in October 2020. I shivered as we walked across the parking lot, dead leaves crunching beneath our feet. Mom unlocked the car and tossed her purse in the back. I pulled open the passenger door and slid down into the seat. The first thing I did was turn on the seat warmer.

The leaves were turning brown and falling to the ground. Autumn, the dying breath of summer.

Mom sat down in the driver's seat and closed the door behind her. Lines were etched into the sides of her mouth, and her eyes looked tired — she looked years older than she had yesterday. We sat there for a moment, both staring at the dashboard.

I thought she might say something, but she finally turned the ignition, and the car came to life with a choked rumble. Tinny music leaked out of the car radio and filled the space between us.

I craned my neck a little to look in the rearview mirror. The purse was slumped over in the back seat, as if in defeat. Some of the papers the doctor had given Mom were poking out. I squinted to try to make out the words on the paper. Something about eating disorders in teens. Or, more accurately, ED. That's what it's always abbreviated to.

I glanced over at Mom, nervous to see how she was handling everything so far. Her forehead was all scrunched up in a sad frown. She stared at the road ahead of her. She was biting the inside of her lip. I could tell. It's hard watching the people you love suffer because of you.

Our car wound through the city streets. Outside my window, I soon saw the edge of our neighbourhood — the greenspace and a bench.

The bench.

Even in the detached haze the hospital had left me in, the memories came rushing back.

Cold winter nights, fingers intertwined . . .

I blinked a couple times, pulling myself back to reality. It's crazy how some memories never seem to age. Loneliness, I've learned, is like a song. Sometimes you forget it exists, until you hear its soft melody in the most obscure places.

Eventually, we pulled into the driveway. The sky was darkening, twilight falling over the city.

The moment we got inside, Mom and I went different ways. By the crestfallen way she watched me turn to run up the stairs, I could tell she didn't want me to hide in my room for the rest of the night. It was for the best, though — I'd already upset her, and if she wanted to ask questions and I wanted to answer them honestly, she'd only get more upset. She'd been guessing I was sick for a while, but still, the reality of all this was probably crashing down on her.

I closed my bedroom door, locked it, and flopped down on my bed, staring blankly at the ceiling.

A gentle knocking at my door. "Charlotte?" Mom said quietly.

I didn't answer.

"I've got these papers." I heard them rustle. "I'm gonna go over them. Tomorrow we're going to have to start making some changes."

Changes. *That's an interesting way to disguise 'eating more,'* I thought.

"I'll let you rest. Goodnight," Mom added after a bit, and I heard her footsteps disappear down the hallway.

I closed my eyes and pretended I was healthy.

I closed my eyes and pretended that I wouldn't run out of time; I wouldn't have to go into treatment.

I pretended I could be immortal.

That's how I got to this moment. Alone in the darkness, wondering when I fell from healthy into the dark crevice of where I am now. It's hard to say for sure, maybe about six months ago.

The truth is, I don't know exactly when he came.

Who is he?

His name is Ed.

He used to count my reps, back when I had the energy to exercise.

He lies next to me in the middle of the night when I can't sleep.

He watches me as I eat.

He's in Instagram posts; he's in advertisements.

He's in mirrors.

I was alone in my head, until one day I realized I wasn't. Now he's in here with me.

THE LANKY BOY

In the middle of the night, as I lie sprawled across my bed in light sleep, I feel a breeze blowing my dyed-blonde hair against my face.

I don't remember leaving my bedroom window open.

A strong gust of wind bursts through the window, and my curtains flap against the walls like a panicked bird trying to escape. My heart jumps with adrenaline, and in a second I'm on my feet beside my bed.

The wind recedes to a calm, warm night breeze that gently billows the curtains. I'm not sure where this heat is coming from — it was freezing when I walked from the hospital to Mom's car.

I see no immediate danger, and my pulse calms, my jitters subside. I rub my eyes. I've always had a shitty record for sleeping. Only when I pull the palms of my hands away from my face do I notice it: the view from my bedroom window has completely changed.

Before, my window looked out to a busy alleyway crowded with aging houses. Now, I overlook a grassy meadow from atop a hill. A thick, ancient oak tree sits in gently swaying grasses. Faint chirp of crickets. Off to the side of the meadow, there's a bench.

I lean against the frame of my open window and squint at it. It's not just any bench.

It's *the* bench.

I breathe in deeply, filling my lungs with the fresh scent of the night — earthy, floral, reminiscent of rain.

Something about all this seems otherworldly.

A shuffling noise. I look down to the grass two stories below my window.

There's a boy.

He has hollow cheeks and a sharp jawline. His pearl-white skin glows in the darkness of the night; his body is long and lanky. Bones are razor blades beneath his skin. His proportions are so unusual it's almost hard to believe he's real. And this gives him a sort of captivating divinity.

What's he doing here? I open my dry mouth; no words come out.

My heartbeat quickens in my chest. I'm afraid of this strange boy. But there's something else too . . . An unspoken, inexplicable connection.

An energy flashes around me — fight-or-flight. Instead, I lean further out the window. I need to be closer to him.

The breeze lifts for a moment, brushing his black, middle-parted hair slightly before it falls back to the sides of his face.

His gaze holds mine, his eyes grey, milky blue.

I jolt upright in bed, gasping. A thin sheen of cold sweat glistens on my forehead. I wipe my face with the sleeve of my pajama shirt.

My arm is still tightly wrapped around my teddy bear.

My eyes dart to my window. Outside, the dreary city alleyway. *Whoa! That was one hell of a dream.*

I can't stop shaking. It takes several minutes for my body to calm down. I'm about to nestle back into my covers when something catches my eye — something I hadn't noticed before.

My window is open a crack. I stare at it with wide eyes, and gingerly slide from my bed to go close it.

I *could've sworn* I'd *closed it.* I pull it fully shut and flip the lock. It's hard to be sure though. I could've easily forgotten. It's not the sort of thing I usually think about.

Before I go back to bed, I inspect the ground below. End up staring out my window at the city for a long, long while.

RIBS

The next morning, brushing my hair, I notice how much of it comes out with each stroke. I hold out the brush and stare at a brittle clump. Self-consciously, I run a hand through my hair. But when I pull my hand out, more is interwoven between my fingers.

It's okay, I try to tell myself. *There's still enough there.* I imagine balding at fifteen, and feel a brief second of horror, then scoff at the idea. *No, that's ridiculous. I won't lose more — it was just tangled.* I yank the hair out of my brush, trash it, and place the brush back down on the bathroom countertop before heading downstairs.

My brother Parker, who's thirteen, two years younger than me, sits at the dining room table. His bulky, noise-cancelling headphones rest around his neck, and he shovels scrambled eggs into his mouth with a fork in one hand while he scrolls on his phone with the other, pausing only to gulp a tall glass of orange juice. Fluffy, uncombed brown hair hangs down to his bushy eyebrows. When I pass by him, he looks up with dark blue eyes, yawns. "Morning."

"Good morning."

Water runs through the pipes as someone showers upstairs — probably Dad, at this time in the morning.

I'm quickly making my morning smoothie, trying to finish it before Mom comes down so she can't see all the ingredients I'm skipping.

"I've got some new ideas for how you can bulk up your smoothies," Mom declares as she enters the kitchen.

Too late.

"I like my smoothies the way they are." I continue with what I'm doing.

Behind me, Mom opens the fridge. Places a container of yogurt on the counter in front of me. I gently shove it away. Mom persists, gets out a measuring cup and begins to spoon the thick vanilla yogurt into it.

"Mom! What are you doing?"

"Getting some yogurt ready for your smoothie."

"Well, stop it," I say. "You're wasting yogurt. I don't want it." I squeeze a small frozen banana into my smoothie.

Mom grabs the measuring cup by the handle and reaches it towards my cup. I deftly slide it away.

"I said stop," I say firmly.

"You have to, Charlotte. You don't have a choice." If she's trying for empathy, I'm too anxious to pick up on it. She reaches out again.

This time, I lightly push her away, a hand on each shoulder. Tears fill my eyes. She tries to move around me, but I shove her again, harder this time. "Don't touch it!" My voice rising.

Parker scrambles to put on his headphones and bolts for the stairs.

My only job is to protect my smoothie. Nothing else matters. I can't let her sugary yogurt into it.

Mom keeps pushing forwards, and I keep shoving her, harder and harder and harder. "Please! Stop it!" I beg, breaking down in sobs.

My pushes are strong. I'm physically weak, but fear has power.

I hear myself screaming, can feel my own mouth spewing hurtful words to keep her away. "I'll hurt you! I'll fucking hurt you!" It doesn't matter that she's my mom. *Just get away get away get the fuck away.*

Defeated. I watch the cup of yogurt plop into my smoothie; my shoulders sag. My entire face wet with tears. A pit of dread settles into my stomach. I'm going to have to eat that.

Mom gets out the handheld blender from a cabinet and gives it to me. I hold it in my hands for a second before attaching its cord to the outlet in the wall and blending the polluted contents of my smoothie.

My heart is pounding as I watch it churn in the cup. Tears drip from my cheeks.

I don't want to be here I don't want to be here I don't want to be here.

Mom tries to put her hand on my shoulder. "You're doing great."

Great? I'm doing GREAT? Something inside of me wakes up; something rageful, accusing, aggressive. I feel heat rise to my cheeks.

Ed joins the conversation. 'She's mocking you,' he explains. 'After making you suffer to get smaller, she's now making you suffer to get bigger again.'

All she does is make me suffer. Suffer suffer suffer.

I turn off the blender, yank the cord out of the outlet. Pull it from the smoothie, toss it to the floor. Bits of smoothie splattering across the hardwood like blood from a gunshot wound. My crying is silent but hard —

I'm suffocating in it. I manage to form three coherent words through my gasping sputtering choking: "Clean it up."

Everything is quiet. Neither of us moves for a second. Mom looks shocked, but shock burning away to rage. She bends down and picks up the discarded blender.

In a sudden, violent motion, she smashes it down against the counter's edge.

Stunned, I stare at her.

"How's that, Charlotte!" she screams. I back up. She slams it down again. It shatters into fragments of white plastic. "How do you like that!"

Fear tightens my chest; I spin around and sprint out of the kitchen. For some reason, though, I grab my smoothie before I leave. Breakfast in hand, I stumble up the stairs and to my bedroom, where I slam my bedroom door, rush to the mirror, plunk the smoothie down on my bookshelf, and frantically pull my shirt over my head. Only when I see my reflection do I calm down.

Time stops in the face of beauty; time stops in the face of suffering.

The human skeleton is just so beautiful. It carries all the elegance of an angel.

The structure of the bones, ethereal architecture. Of course I would want to see them; want to see the intricate ridges of my ribs jutting out of my torso, wrapping around from my solar plexus to my spine. The ribs fight against my skin in an attempt to burst through, with a power that makes feeble skin sink between them. On my chest, rib bones splay out like the wings of a butterfly. Seeing myself like this brings peace, serenity. I could stare at these ribs forever; they're my favourite of my bones, by far.

At that moment, I know I still have control. Everything is okay.

For now.

But maybe, just maybe, I can convince myself that now is all I need.

Mom storms upstairs as well, but instead of entering my room heads down the hall to her own room. Her door slams. Thumping and cracking. She's breaking something. Clothing hangers?

I sniffle, wipe my nose. The tears are different now — they're not hot tears of panic caused by food. They're tears of horror.

Look what I've done.

Look what I've done.

Look what I've done.

Look how I've let my mom down.

I raise the cup to my lips and take a sip through quivering breaths. It tastes like shit. The vanilla yogurt doesn't go at all with the chocolate protein shake. It's horrible.

I slump down on my bed. I wish this wasn't the problem that it is for me. I wish I didn't have to do this to my family. I listen to the smashing from my mom's room, sip at my smoothie, tears dripping into the cup. I can't do it. I try, but I don't end up drinking very much. Such a simple thing — the mere act of raising the cup and swallowing — but I can't. I can't do anything right, it seems.

This morning, my dad drives me to school. Before we leave, I drink lots of water and dab at my eyes, hoping to make it less obvious that I've been crying. We don't talk. We listen to the news as we drive. I wonder what he thinks of his own daughter.

In the distance, the skyscrapers. I've never been much of a city girl, but Calgary has its perks. Sun bursts through the slits of space between the city skyscrapers. I lean my head against the window as the city passes by, still caught in its innocence of morning haze.

WHEN I WAS YOUNGER

Everything I felt, I felt at the extremes. I glowed with love for my parents, or felt a rainstorm of sadness when I had to say goodbyes.

I was lucky enough to be born into a well-off family; money was never an issue. My dad worked a very intense job downtown. When I did get to see him, he was usually in a professional suit. He looked so smart and sophisticated, and I was proud to be his daughter.

Unfortunately, though, I didn't get to see him much. I missed him.

A lot.

When he was at his busiest, he would miss breakfast, lunch, and dinner. When he finally walked through the door, sometimes his frustrations from work had stalked him home to spend the evening with our family. He would growl, and swear, and give me his harrowing, signature glare, with patchy eyebrows glowering and eyes bulging, filled with unpredictable anger. When I didn't miss him, I was scared of him.

I still loved him, though. And I know that he still loved me, too. He just had a hard time expressing love.

Then, there was my mom — an idol to me. She also worked a busy job downtown, but not quite as busy as Dad's, so she still got to be a big part of my life. As a little five-year-old, I wanted to be with her always — to protect her from the dangers of the world. This, I believed, was my responsibility. I couldn't imagine a world without her.

As a result, when she got mad at me, instead of running off, I'd follow her around the house like a shadow, wanting no space between us.

When she dropped me off at preschool, I was always in tears. I never wanted to say goodbye. It didn't matter that she would be back at the end of the day — all that mattered was the present. What if something happened to her while she was gone? What if she *didn't* come back?

I wanted to be perfect for my parents. Still do. Perfect grades, perfect relationships, perfect attitudes — the perfect daughter.

But perfect, it seems, is unattainable. I'm always so close, *almost*, as if I could reach out and grab on to the delicate, shining purity that is perfection. Every time, though, it slips through my fingers.

SPRAY PAINT AND RHINESTONES

The next Saturday evening, I'm on a city transit bus, jolted by the occasional pothole and speedbump. The girl sitting beside me, by the window, surveys the passing city outside with honey-brown eyes outlined with striking black eyeliner. Silver eyeshadow dusts her eyelids. Dark brown hair is pinned back from her face with neon hairclips.

Olivia — the one part of my life that resembles some sort of teenage normalcy. One earphone is in her ear, and the other is in mine. Indie rock lights up my mind.

She turns to me. "So, what're we picking up this time?"

Every once in a while, we take the bus down to the nearby strip mall for art supplies. I don't take art nearly as seriously as Olivia does, but I still like wandering the aisles.

"Maybe some coloured pens? Gotta make my science notes *aesthetic*," I say. "You?"

She narrows her eyes for a moment, thinking. "What about those little rhinestones?"

"For what? Scrapbooking?"

"Well, yeah, but I'd stick them on my face." She points to the corners of her eyes eagerly. "Right here."

"I like it!"

I can tell from the way her eyes scrunch up that she's smiling beneath her mask.

A new song starts on the earphones. A raw balance of punchy, vintage electric guitar and soft vocals. "Oh my god, I love this song," I say.

"Right! Isn't it pretty?"

For the rest of the bus ride, we listen to the song in appreciative silence and stare out the window. The bus rolls up to our strip mall, and we get off. Olivia's platform Doc Martens hit the sidewalk with a thump.

"Thank you!" she calls to the driver as the bus doors close behind us, slinging her backpack over her shoulder.

The air smells fresh with twilight.

Soon, we're exploring the aisles of Michaels, the art supplies store. "We're closing in twenty," a tired-looking employee sighs, then disappears to some other aisle.

Olivia buzzes from shelf to shelf, examining sketchbooks and pencil crayons. We pass by a display of paint sample cards, an explosion of colour—little rectangles in every hue imaginable. She glances down the empty aisle, then stuffs a handful in her pocket.

Followed by Olivia, I meander down to the scrapbook area. Pick up a small black photo album. Maybe I can print out my body checks and store them here.

"Thinking about starting a memory album?" Olivia peers over my shoulder.

"Yeah," I say. *Something like that.*

She snatches some rhinestones from an adjacent shelf, mumbling to herself, "These are perfect." She turns to me. "Anything else you wanna check out?"

"I don't think so," I say. We start making our way back to the front of the store, winding through the aisles. "Wait."

She stops. "Yeah?"

The shelves in front of me are stocked with tall, shining cylinder cans, each with a different coloured lid.

Olivia comes back to examine them, picking one up and reading the label.

"Spray paint?"

"Yep." I grin.

"What're you thinking?" she asks, intrigued.

I pause for a second, then decide, "I'm gonna buy some."

She grins back. "Me too, then."

We root through the cans, looking for the right paints.

Reaching into the selection, her eyes light up. Her hand re-emerges with a can with a periwinkle lid. "This," she says. "This is the one."

"Love it," I agree. "It suits you."

Hidden deep on the shelf—a glint of deep crimson. I lean in. Pull it out.

Olivia steps beside me, squinting at the label. "Blood red," she reads. "It's very . . . distinctive."

I wonder if the blood inside me is this shade.

"I'm getting it," I say.

She nods approvingly.

By the time we step outside, it's already dark. "Are you gonna tell me what we're actually planning to do with these?" Olivia asks, tossing her canister in her hand as we walk back to the bus stop.

I look at her. "Felony."

I admire the way my blood-red canister gleams in the streetlights. The photo album and rhinestones are in Olivia's backpack. We don't have to wait long for a bus to come, though it's one of the final pickups of the night. It stops with a hiss by the curb, and we hop on, sit down at the very back.

"Any idea where we're going with these?" Olivia asks, glancing down at her own spray paint when the bus gets moving.

"What about the back of the 7-Eleven? You know, the one by my house?" I suggest.

"Gritty," she says, handing me an earphone. "I'm in." The comfort of the music sparks through us. She rests her head on my shoulder.

Several stops later, I push the stop button, and the bus pulls over at the next bus shelter.

We take off running.

"How are you so fast!" I call out. Olivia is several feet in front of me, even in her heavy boots. She laughs joyously.

The night air is cold, and I can already tell my nose is turning pink. The moon is a pale sliver in the sky, and we race between the bright lights glowing from the streetlamps.

Charged by exhilaration, we sprint around a corner, into the alleyway behind the 7-Eleven—empty and unlit, strewn only with the odd wrapper or bag. Sketchier than I thought.

"Is this safe?" I ask nervously, still out of breath and light-headed from running so fast.

Olivia scans the alleyway. "Yeah. There's two of us, anyway."

I nod. *It's too late to chicken out.* "Let's do this."

We flick off the lids, take off the seal.

"You shake it, right? That's what they do on TV," Olivia says.

"Right," I say, brandishing my canister. Paint shoots from the valve, drips down the brick wall like velvety red blood. I wave my arm along the wall, stretching and crouching with each stroke. Put my hand on my hip. Step back.

A gigantic C.

"That's *so cool*," Olivia says. She aims her canister at the wall, and a spray of serene, icy periwinkle bursts forward. When she pulls her arm away, there's an equally large O beside my C.

"Here." I add a plus sign between the two letters. The softness of the periwinkle melts in with the violent boldness of the red.

The bland brick wall comes alive with our paint. Explosions of unapologetic colour.

Olivia tries what I can only assume to be a self-portrait, but it ends up as a disjointed blob.

"Abstract art, maybe?" I suggest, looking at it.

"That's generous." She laughs.

I paint a heart; she adds periwinkle highlights.

There's something satisfying about vandalism—with a simple mark of spray paint, you make a tiny fragment of yourself immortal.

We click the lids back on to the canisters and throw them in Olivia's backpack. She gestures towards the 7-Eleven. "Wanna get something to drink?"

"Yeah."

We stroll around to the front of the convenience store. Harsh white light streams out of the windows, like a fluorescent star in the night. The lit-up *Open* sign flickers as we step inside. They have a decent selection of Monster energy drinks. Olivia picks the one with the most artistic design—a purple dragon slinking along the side of the can. I pick the zero-calorie option.

One could argue that energy drinks are a bad idea when you're severely underweight, but whatever. We step back into the night. My Monster makes a hissing sound as I pop the tab open.

"Cheers," I say, and we knock our cans together. I raise mine to my lips, and the flavour of grapefruit and strawberries floods my mouth.

The night sky is remarkably clear, inviting us to disappear into it. Olivia's earrings jingle as we walk. Occasional cars pass by us in rushes of wind.

A strange thought enters my mind, pushing through the peaceful rhythm of our footsteps and distant rush of traffic. I still haven't told Olivia about my situation. I'm not medically stable; what if something happens to me? I hate the thought of leaving her alone, confused as to what's going on.

"I have something to tell you," I say, watching the cars pass.

"Yeah?" She looks over at me; I look back. There's a hint of concerned curiosity in her eyes.

How do I say this?

If only there was a way to explain everything without explaining Ed.

I tell her about this whole mess that is my illness. She doesn't look surprised as I speak, which catches me slightly off guard. Sometimes I forget my darkest secret is visible to those who take the time to be observant enough. Normal, healthy people don't look like I do. "I just thought you should know in case anything . . . happens."

"I know a lot has changed for you, Charlotte," she says.

"You know what hasn't changed, though? Who you are as a person."

A pit in my stomach. I bite the inside of my cheek.

My parents see me differently. I can tell from the way they nervously glance at me while I eat; the exasperation on their faces when they speak to me.

I don't blame them — I *feel* different now.

I'm not the same.

I look at Olivia — so thoughtful, but so unaware. *How long until she finds out she's wrong?*

She takes a sip from her drink and recoils, her face scrunching up.

"Not a good flavour?" I ask, laughing.

"What is this?" she says, looking at the can. "Tastes like battery acid."

As we chat and joke, I forget the way I screamed at my mom over yogurt and the tormented way she screamed back — the way I let my parents down over and over again. This is as close as I've gotten to feeling healthy; normal.

At *this moment*, it's just us, the night and our drinks. Part of me secretly wishes we would never get home, just keep walking together. I'd like to live in this moment in a constant loop — avoiding the hardships of tomorrow, living infinitely in the moment.

GUSTS OF WIND IN
A PERFECT STORM

It *takes an unlikely set of circumstances* for a tornado to form. To start, there must be enough moisture in the air. From there, the vapour condenses into liquid; a lifting mechanism in the atmosphere causes air to rise, which makes it expand and cool. Warmer air near the earth's surface and colder air high in the atmosphere results in instability, with the warm air pushing upward. Only with sharp changes in wind speed or direction will that updraft start to spin, but if it does, you've got a natural disaster that has the potential to destroy everything it comes across.

Eating disorders are similar. Expose a human being to a set of events that happen to fit together in a way that is so horribly perfect, and the unlucky person spins out, at its mercy.

I *remember the first time* I really paid attention to my weight. I was nine years old, with a sudden, strong dislike for my body. It lasted about a year, then went away, temporarily. I remember taking off all my clothes before getting into the shower, and stepping on the scale we used to keep in the bathroom. I'd stare down at the number from above my belly, bloated from dinner, and something inside of me would deflate, crushing disappointment flooding me as the number stared back. I stepped off the scale and turned around to stare in the mirror, ashamed. I didn't really understand what a normal weight was for a girl of my age — all I knew was that eighty seemed like a huge number. My mind was already a collage of pictures and comments — my mom and her friends — "well don't *you* look nice and skinny!" — magazines promoting the secret to a perfect, frail beach body. Even at nine, I'd already come to understand that no one wants a big number when they stand on a scale.

I remember a time when I had a great relationship with food and my body. But I also remember some of the unkind things that were said to me because of that.

Throughout junior high, I was friends with a girl named Mara. She was funny, but occasionally switched over to rude. She also loved to flex the fact that she rarely ate breakfast.

It was the middle of Grade 9, a couple of months before the global pandemic closed everything down. Mara, Olivia, a few other friends, and I were at someone's house with bowls of takeout poke. I'd been hungry; Olivia and I finished before Mara even got halfway through. I didn't even notice until Mara stared at my bowl with wide, judgy eyes. She then glanced over at Olivia's. "You've already finished?" she gawked. "Man, you guys are *pigs.*"

"Hey!" Olivia shot an irritated glance at her. I didn't think about it much at the time. But later, when things started to get worse, it was all that I *could* think about whenever I was eating. It happened insidiously. I began going through my daily life, thinking how much better I would look with an eating disorder.

On March 15 COVID-19 was still nothing more than a distant news story, an intriguing word that lurked in the background, only occasionally mentioned in conversation. That evening, though, we received news that the schools were shutting down. I never went back to any of my Grade 9 classrooms. That's when it all got real; our lifestyle completely changed.

I'd always wanted to be thinner. I'd put it off, though, never having the time or motivation to really commit to changing my body. But now, spending every day at home, I had more than enough time to do whatever I wanted. I chose my goal — to lose weight. Mom was doing it with WeightWatchers. Why couldn't I join her? Surely it would work well for me, too. Why wouldn't healthy eating make my life better? Something inside of me quietly added: *Because skinnier is prettier, right?*

One time I found myself stressed about having a snack when I was hungry. Mom tried to reassure me. "I'm trying to lose weight, so when I'm hungry, maybe I'll have a glass of water. But you don't have to lose, so have an apple."

I had all the time I needed to exercise, too, and I was relentless with it. I never took rest days. I had this mentality that as long as I burned more calories than I ate, the day was a success. I was working towards a goal.

I just hadn't yet realized what a sinister goal it was.

I got into running and biking, and joined my mom's hardcore diet — high fibre, high protein, low everything else. We did it together. Somewhere along the line, something changed for me, though. It wasn't a fun way to connect with my mom anymore. I was trapped in her dieting habits. Ed admired her.

All this fear about a global pandemic, about deaths

across the world and everything about our lives turned upside down — when I focused on my goal, none of it seemed to affect me anymore. I was committed to losing weight; I spotlighted it. It was a wonderful distraction.

Plus, the internet was exploding with people with the same goal — weight loss! YouTube videos of at-home exercises popped up, *what-I-eat-in-a-day* posts on Instagram. The community of dieters in the world grew like never before. The goal of losing weight was everywhere I looked.

Dad's been known to make fun of people's bodies. In the checkout line while we're at the grocery store, he'll see an overweight person. Later, when we're in the car, he'll make some stupid jab, like, "Maybe wide-ass shouldn't have been buying all those cookies." He'll defend himself, if Mom gets on his case, saying that he makes fun of people who are too thin and too fit, too. One could argue that just makes him triple the jerk.

In May, the friend group was hanging out at Olivia's house. We were all sitting on the lawn in her backyard, socially distanced. One of the girls, Rebecca, had brought some cupcakes with her. They looked delicious, and sure enough, they were. Everyone had had one, and there were lots left, so I asked Rebecca if I could have another.

"Yeah, for sure!" Rebecca said.

As I reached for another one and took a bite, Mara exclaimed, "You're having *another* one?" That hurt.

When we got to Grade 10 at Western Canada High School, Mara split off to join another group. I was secretly relieved. She never understood how much her words affected me.

Ten pounds lost.

Every morning, when my brother and Dad had bacon and toast, my mom and I had a quarter cup of oats each. The bland oats floated in a shallow pool of tap water. When I was eating them, I felt like I was connecting with Mom. They quickly became my favourite meal.

Every week, I got a little thinner. The weeks started to build up; I continued to shrink. Just like that, I had an emotional outlet — starvation. It really was the perfect storm.

That's when the dreams started.

They started calm — pleasant, even. Sitting on the grass with Olivia, an assortment of convenience-store snacks set up in a little picnic. Almost all my dreams revolved around food; not stressful, just a strange recurrence.

Twenty pounds off my original weight.

They got more bizarre. Sitting down at a long table of people, perhaps in a cafeteria somewhere, only to see how little everyone else was eating — only a few carrots. I looked down at my plate — a heaping pile of pasta in a white sauce. The girl next to me glanced over with a sour expression, and slid a seat away.

I detested speedbumps, obsessed over how my remaining fat jiggled with each jolt.

A missing period should've been the red flag, but I'd been on continuous birth control since Grade 8 to manage acne. Since I didn't take a week away from the pill every month to menstruate, there was no definitive moment to tell me parts of my body were shutting down.

Eventually, I started to think that something wasn't right. I realized this far before anyone else. I lived with unease that there was something deeper in me beyond my eating and exercising habits, something dark and driven. More than anything, I wanted to be wrong.

But I was right.

Thirty pounds.

The dreams turned into nightmares, and plagued me on the regular. A bake sale outside my school. A table, set up with brownies, cupcakes, and cookies — left unattended. I sprinted towards it, sobbing in desperation. *This is it*, I thought as I stumbled. *This is my only chance.*

Icing, smudged across my cheeks and hands, my shirt covered in crumbs. All the baked goods — gone. *What could I eat next?*

I heard an irritated voice: "Hey!" A volunteering mom stormed towards me, daggers in her eyes. People started stepping out from behind corners, bushes, trees; they stared at me with piercing eyes.

I woke up with tears on my face, hyperventilating. It took me several moments to realize it had just been a dream; only when I realized I hadn't actually eaten any of that food did I start to calm down.

"I've been having dreams," I told my mom the next morning.

She was flipping through a trashy magazine on the couch, still in her pajamas. "About what?" she asked, without looking up.

I took a deep breath. "Food."

"Huh," she said, pausing. "Now that you mention it, I think I'm ready for breakfast." She left to make herself some oatmeal.

Several days later, I cried after eating my dad's grilled cheese.

Mom noticed. "What's wrong?"

"I don't know, the cheese is just really freaking me out." I wiped at my eyes.

She patted my shoulder, and did nothing else for weeks.

My mom eventually took me to see the family doctor. I think it took her so long because she didn't want to accept that her suspicions might be reality.

"Tell me what you eat in a day." Dr. Vernon was an older man with circular glasses, thinning hair, and sharp facial features.

I listed the meals to him. I ate the bare minimum. The only foods that passed my mouth were the low-calorie items approved by WeightWatchers.

"And how much do you exercise?"

"Quite a bit. I usually run about ten kilometres a day, plus shadowboxing sometimes."

Dr. Vernon thought my exercising was healthy, and my good diet impressive.

Eating disorders, I know now, have no particular look or habit associated with them. Someone can appear 'healthy,' but be very sick, indeed.

Instead of being saved from my illness, I was praised for it.

"Eat some nuts," he said. "Try to incorporate avocado and olive oil into your cooking."

From the corner of his office, my mom nodded.

I nodded, too, without any anticipation of following his advice.

It turns out Mom called him later that month, as she got increasingly worried. She asked him to put me on the waiting list for the Calgary eating disorder ward. Our family had no support system, and she was desperately trying to find help. Weeks later, when she called the eating disorder ward, they said my name had never been put on it.

Dr. Vernon hadn't believed her.

I stopped taking my birth control, and sure enough, my period was gone.

Forty pounds.

Thanks, doc. In the meantime, Mom started taking me to the hospital every week to get my vitals taken.

I can close my eyes, even now, and imagine the violent, powerful tornado in my head, wreaking havoc on my mind, sweeping up everything I thought I knew about myself and tearing it apart.

PREJUDICE

My family and I are out for a walk. It's a beautiful day, but I can't seem to pay attention to any of it. All I can think about is food. There's a big, knotted tangle of stress obscuring me from the rest of my mind.

I try taking deep breaths — anything to ground me in the moment, to keep me here in the present, not living in an endless loop of worrying thoughts.

Ding!

The tinny sound of a bike bell rings out from behind me. My parents, Parker, and I step to the edge of the sidewalk. A larger woman on an electric bike whirs past us.

Cool! I think. I've always wanted to try an electric bike. They look so fun.

I glance over at my dad when I hear sniggering.

When the woman crosses over to the next block and eventually leaves our view, he mutters, "An electric bike? Might not be the best choice for her. She looks like she could use some exercise."

My mom swats at him, and he stops talking, but there's no way to unhear what he said. I bite the inside of my lip to keep myself from tearing up. He'd said it like clockwork. *It's what people think.*

I don't want people to look at me and think that. And they will, I know they will — when I'm not skinny anymore. No one will see me the same way. Ed never fails to remind me. Everyone else is too polite to let it show, though my dad occasionally lets it slip. People will see your weight and pretend they know all about you — your eating and exercising habits, your self-control. Everything.

What do I want people to believe about me? I don't know. I want them to think I'm pretty. I want them to be impressed by my willpower. I want them to say, "I wish I was as thin as that girl." And they do.

They always do.

A DISTANT THOUGHT

I'm slumped in the passenger seat of my mom's car as she drives me from school to an appointment at the hospital to check my vitals and get an EKG scan done. We drive in silence, listening to the radio. It's been a while since it happened, but I still hope she forgives me for the smoothie incident.

My back is a painting of bruises after being in school — there's no fat on my body to protect my hard bones from the rigid back of the cheap school chairs. Bruises spot up my spine, each lower vertebrae leaving its mark; they faintly streak the lengths of my ribs. It hurts.

"I've started looking at hospitalization," my mom announces, breaking the silence.

I'm too tired to discuss this. I just want to go home and go to bed. Still, the distant idea of a hospital is somewhat amusing.

My condition isn't that bad. She won't really do it. It's just a way to scare me into eating more.

I'm too focused on surviving the present to think about the future. It all seems so far away.

"I'm going to be talking about it with Dr. Vernon," she adds.

Ha! Good luck with that! Get ready for a referral to the FUCKING BULK NUT SECTION OF SUPERSTORE. For as long as Dr. Vernon is the only medical professional involved in this situation, I'm free to enjoy Ed's company for as long as I please — forever.

I HOPE YOU KNOW

I've never been this cold in my life.

I'm sitting in psychology class, bundled up in a short-sleeved shirt under a long-sleeved shirt under a hoodie under a winter jacket, and I'm freezing. Heating packets are grasped tightly in my cold hands, but my body seems unable to absorb the heat. I wish I could curl up in the fetal position to conserve it. The worst part is that I still have a long day of torturous freezing ahead of me.

Wearing this many layers is the exact opposite of fashionable, and I can't help but feel self-conscious. I'm in a high school class, and I look like I'm partaking in an Antarctic expedition.

In a weak attempt to fit in with the rest of the high school crowd, I've drawn winged liner over my eyes and streaked my lashes with mascara. Mascara seems to make everyone else look so pretty. Why isn't it working for me? Mine looks too clumpy. I wish I could just slink away.

At least I don't know anyone here. The teacher drones on. It's mostly just kids from the grade above me. The only girl I know sits on the other side of the room. And she . . . well, we haven't talked in quite a while.

I've been pretty good at psych, so far. The teacher keeps going on about mental illness, but, hey, my first-hand experience has already got me covered.

My phone vibrates in my jacket pocket. I sneakily slide it out, glance down. It's a text.

From a girl named Jade.

The only girl here I know.

I glance across the room at her, but her eyes stay fixed to the phone in her lap. I open the text, and it's as if she read my mind.

I hope you know you don't need makeup.

MICHELLE

I'm sitting cross-legged on a couch in the waiting room of a therapy clinic. It's actually a bungalow, but they've renovated it so each room is like an office. It smells like cinnamon incense. Body positivity posters hang on every wall, and 'smooth jazz' plays from a speaker somewhere. I feel awkward.

"Charlotte?"

I jump a little. I guess I was really getting into the smooth jazz.

There's a woman in the doorway. Light brown hair. Blue eyes peer from above a black disposable mask.

"I'm Michelle. It's nice to meet you."

"Nice to meet you, too." I'm not being particularly genuine, but that's what you say when you meet someone new and you want to be polite.

"Come on in." She gestures for me to follow her.

We walk into a brightly lit office, and she closes the door behind her.

And so, Michelle enters my life.

"We're going to talk about a lot of things, and food doesn't have to be one of them," she explains, seating herself gracefully in the grey armchair. She's wearing a beige cardigan and black skinny jeans. Diamonds glint from her ears. "A lot of girls are relieved to hear that."

I stare at her.

If we're not talking about food, though, what are we talking about? Is food, or lack thereof, not the whole reason I ended up here?

Still, I nod.

As far as first impressions go, she acts quite nice.

Ed knows what she's doing, though. She wants me to gain weight, to throw all my hard work out the window. It's Ed and me against the world. And she's just another person making up the world.

She looks at me with a sort of grounded calm as she talks about the clinic. "Identifying unhealthy patterns . . . Rewiring the brain to develop new behaviours . . ." Her eyes look thoughtful. Most practices, she tells me, hold therapy sessions online due to the pandemic. But because of the dire state of their clients, this clinic has some of them come in person. "It builds a more personal relationship between you and me," she explains.

Is there a chance that I could come to like this woman? I know what Ed would say, but where does Ed end and I start?

I suppose it's only fair of me to give her an opportunity.

'*Watch yourself,*' Ed warns, so I watch Michelle's eyes and physical gestures very closely, scanning for any details that might give something away. I'm aware she's probably doing the same with me; I carefully regulate how much information I inadvertently give her.

Control means everything in situations like this. I would know.

SPARKLER

That evening — a gentle knocking at my bedroom door.
"Yes?" I say, looking up from my homework.

The door creaks open, and I can see Parker's eye —
navy, like the night sky — through the crack.

"Come in."

He opens the door all the way and steps inside.
"Wanna go to the park?"

I glance to my window. The sky's overcast. Fallen
leaves rustle through the alleyway, riding a chilled breeze.

I'm gonna freeze, I think. But there's a hopeful excitement in Parker's eyes. I smile. "Sure."

Parker's wearing a long-sleeved shirt; I'm wearing my
winter jacket. Goosebumps rise on my arms beneath the
layer of down. The rhythm of our footsteps against the
sidewalk fills the air. A dusty-brown cat sprints across
the road and onto the sidewalk, stares at us with cloudy
green eyes. It squeezes through an opening beneath a
fence and disappears.

I lose myself in the familiarity of Parker's bubbly
voice as he speaks. Just thirteen years old, he's untouched
by adulthood, barely even touched by adolescence. He
talks about his video games, his vinyl figure collection,
his manga. I nod and ask the occasional question, diving
him deeper into a passionate speech.

Parker — sunset orange, boisterous laughter, playful
summer afternoons. All the energy adults try — unsuccess-
fully — to harness; all the boyishness songs try to capture.

The park by our house is quiet when we arrive.

"Swings?" Parker suggests.

"Definitely," I agree.

We sit there, side by side. A bird caws in the distance. Above us, there's a small break in the clouds; the sun peeks through.

"You know what's crazy?" he says.

"What?"

"We don't have a secret handshake. We should totally have come up with one by now."

I grin. "Let's make one, then."

A flurry of high-fives, fist-bumps, and hand-waving ensues.

The two of us just click like puzzle pieces. We may look different — he's shorter and tan, while I'm taller and pale — but I bet if there was a way to see our minds, they would look similar.

Or they would've — before Ed, at least.

Parker throws a frisky punch at my shoulder.

"What was that!"

"Part of the handshake!" He laughs.

"Yeah, I don't think so," I say with a chuckle. "This is way too complicated — how are we gonna remember this?"

"You're right, we won't. What if we just did a bro-hug?"

"Does that even count as a handshake?"

His eyes gleam. "Sure it does, if we say so."

You're like a sparkler — sudden, dazzling, bright. More than any ordinary sparkler, though — if suspended high in the sky on a clear night, you'd look like a star.

Parker starts pumping his legs. Up he goes, putting more and more distance between himself and the ground, then quickly rushing back down towards it as he sweeps forwards and backwards. He reminds me of myself two years ago, filled with curiosity and endless energy.

The swing seat is crushing the sides of my pelvis, but I try to do the same. After several pumps, though, it hurts too much — I'm going to end up with bruises. From the ground, I watch him swing so high it's like his feet dip into the sky.

He's soaring! I think, while gravity drags me down from the stars.

THE MYSTERIOUS GIRL

Four days later, I collapse into my bed.

The day had been going alright until I got home from school. After I got into another food-related fight with my parents — they're happening more often now — and ran upstairs, I stood on the landing around the corner, hidden from their view.

I listened to them. I knew I was going to regret hearing what they were going to say. Knew it was going to hurt. But I wanted a snippet of what was really going on in their heads, in its rawest, truest form, so I eavesdropped anyway.

"I don't know how we're going to do this at home." Mom sighed. Her voice sounded like a string wound too tightly. I didn't need to see her to know she was running her hands anxiously through her hair.

"At least it's not cancer," Dad said. "At least we can have control over it."

Control?

I have *no* control over my mind. What place is he in to say *at least it's not?* It's my life, and everything I thought I knew about myself is falling apart. My illness isn't a matter of just putting food down my throat — it runs so much deeper. I bet if I had a physical illness, he'd take it seriously.

I wasn't going to get anything happy out of listening in. I turned on my heel and silently sprinted to my bedroom — a cavity in me, as though my lungs, exhausted from their endless straining, are deflating.

It's still relatively early, but I just want the day to be over. I root through my bedside cabinet until I find some melatonin tablets, flick open the little container and pop one into my mouth, letting its minty flavour melt on to my tongue. That's always been my go-to coping mechanism. *You can't stress if you're not conscious*, I think, pulling the heavy blankets over my thin body.

I don't remember falling asleep, but I'm aware I'm waking up. Startled, my muscles clench. The air sucks out of my lungs.

At the foot of my bed stands a girl. Her face is lit up by the pale light the moon is casting through my window. The first thing I notice is her eyes. They look just like mine — bluish green, like where the ocean hits the beach. But where my features are sharp and definitive, hers appear softer, gentler. She looks about my age. Her eyes dance with . . . what is it? Curiosity? Amusement?

"Who are you? How did you get in?" I ask, stunned. My voice sounds more astonished than scared.

A slight grin tugs at the corners of her mouth.

Suddenly, she spins around and starts running. "Wait, come back!" I shout after her as she disappears into the hallway.

I scramble out from under my blankets and run after her. The house is quiet and still as I run through it, moonlight casting long shadows across the rooms. I'm on the verge of losing sight of her — she keeps slipping out of my view, leaving me with only her hair swishing behind her as she rounds a corner, or her foot as she darts through a doorway.

She's fast, and though I pump my legs with every bit of force I can muster, my body refuses to run at her speed.

Ahead of me, I hear a rush of air as the back door swings open. I see she's left the door open behind her.

I freeze.

Outside, there is no alley. There's a meadow basked in moonlight, with the bench and an ancient oak tree. There's no rumbling and honking of cars, but instead, the lonesome and melodic sound of crickets. From the doorway, I have a perfect view of the girl. She's sprinting straight through the meadow, towards the oak tree, her hair flowing behind her.

With my clothes dishevelled from having fallen asleep in them, I take off running after her. I consider yelling something out to her, but I can barely breathe from such fast running, and I have no air to spare.

When she reaches the thick trunk of the oak tree, she stops. A couple minutes later, I join her. I lean over with my hands on my knees, gasping for breath. The fresh night air fills my lungs.

She is facing the moon, her back to me.

I have so many questions, I can barely collect them to speak.

"Who are you?" I manage to ask again.

The girl turns around to smile at me. "To you," she says, "I am the Mysterious Girl."

I look at her, then around at the meadow we're standing in. "This can't be real. I have to be dreaming." It seems obvious now—how could this not have dawned on me earlier?

But the soft breeze brushes against my face. The long grass sways around my ankles. It all feels so real.

"Who's to say it can't be both?" she says.

"What do you mean?" I ask, bewildered.

The Mysterious Girl walks around to the other side of the oak tree. I follow her, and watch as she reaches up, stretching her arm as far as it will go and curling her fingers around the lowest branch.

"It's been all the rage with philosophers since, like, forever," she says.

From there, she walks her feet up on the trunk and crawls her body on to the branch until she is sitting on it.

"Dreams, illusions, hallucinations. It's always about these strange phenomena, where our senses mislead us." She dangles her feet beneath her and swings them playfully. "So here's the question," she continues. "If we know that this happens sometimes, how do we know it doesn't *always* happen?"

She looks up from her feet to me. "Isn't that interesting?" she asks eagerly.

At a loss for words, I simply nod.

"So now here's another question. This one's yours." She jumps down from the tree branch and lands directly in front of me. "Do things have an objective existence, independent of whether anyone is actually thinking about them?" She taps her temple with her index finger as she adds, "Or is it just all in our heads?"

"I . . . I don't understand," I mumble, picking at my cuticles and frowning.

"That's okay, it was a trick question anyways. There's no way to ever be sure." The Mysterious Girl winks.

"Now that you've said that, would it be totally useless for me to ask where I am?"

"No, not at all. This place does have a name, you know," the Mysterious Girl states matter-of-factly. She takes a couple steps away from me, then throws her arms out to her sides. "I welcome you to *the Deep!*"

"The Deep?"

She nods, and adds, "Population of three."

"And who are these three?" I ask.

"Well, I guess that's not totally true. There are other people, as you might see, but they don't exist here at the same level that we do," she corrects herself.

"What?"

"Don't worry. You'll understand eventually."

I think back to the lanky boy I saw from my window the night previous. "I've been here before," I say. "I saw someone. I wonder if he might have been one of the three?"

Some of the Mysterious Girl's youthful energy seems to fade away for a minute, and a seriousness takes its place. "Describe him," she says flatly.

"Tall. Skinny. Black hair, strange eyes." The image of him remains clear in my memory.

The Mysterious Girl says nothing, but she stares at me with a consequential look in her eyes. I wait for her to speak. She doesn't. I begin to feel uncomfortable.

"You know who the third person is?" she asks abruptly. A grin lights up her face, but there's still something dark deep in her eyes.

"Who?" I respond.

"You, of course!" she exclaims.

"I live here?"

She nods. "You do now."

I feel disoriented. I consider asking her what she means, but so far, her answers have only made me more confused. Instead, I decide to move on to the one question that's been nagging at me. "Who is the boy, though?" I press.

She straightens her posture. "His name is Ed," she answers gravely. "I believe you're already acquainted with him."

UNSPOKEN

In the morning, I splash cold water on my face, as if trying to wash away the residue the dream has left on my mind. About thirty minutes before school starts, I meet up with Olivia behind my house. She grins at me eagerly, mounted on a bicycle. Rhinestones gleam in the corners of her eyes.

I guide my own bicycle out of the garage and join her.

Olivia lives nearby, so we're giving biking to school together a try.

"What did you get up to last night?" I ask as I get on my bike, my hair tousled by a chilly morning breeze. I shiver.

"Math homework," she answers with a sigh.

"That's brutal." I glance back at her. "Ready?"

"Yeah, let's do this!"

We take off, winding through the streets, along roads, and cutting through parks to get to school. A mom walks to her car, followed by two bouncy, rambunctious kids wearing backpacks. A man strolls down the sidewalk with a German shepherd on a leash. The morning air is crisp with autumn. I look up at the bleak grey sky.

It's nice to shake things up from city transit, but my cheeks are stinging from the cold. I try to ignore the burning pain in my bony legs, and briefly miss the muscles I used to have.

This bike ride should be easy. Why am I struggling so much?

It's okay, though, I assure myself. *You look fantastic.*

My body is shivering violently now, fingers starting to go numb. I glance over my shoulder. Olivia's right behind me; I'm holding her up. I try to pump my legs faster, but it's no use.

We start up a hill, with spectacular homes on either side of the road. My legs are screaming in pain. I grit my teeth.

Think of how many calories you're burning, I remind myself for motivation.

The top of the hill still so far; I'm slowing down. My trembling legs.

Almost there . . .

Finally, the top. Here the road gets flatter. I feel like I'm about to collapse from exhaustion. Thankfully, we're coming up on a steep downhill — I wipe the sweat from my face.

"That was a tough one," Olivia says behind me, but I know she's only saying it to make me feel better.

I've never been so weak. We're nearly late. I feel bad for holding Olivia up, but I'm too ashamed to say anything about it, so I don't, and she must feel sympathetic for me, because she doesn't, either.

After school, I bike back home, put my bike in the garage, and head up to my bedroom to start some chemistry homework.

My mom knocks on my door.

"Come in." I look up from my papers.

She creaks it further open and leans against the doorframe with her arms crossed. "I don't think you should bike to school anymore," she says.

"What do you mean?" My voice is sharp.

"It's burning calories we can't afford to lose."

I feel heat flushing my cheeks, and snap, "You can't take that away from me!" Sure, biking burns calories, but that's why I love it so much.

"I won't let you." She sounds almost apologetic.

"Get out!" I scream.

She doesn't yell, though I almost wish she would — a heated reaction, a fight. A chance to unplug the all-consuming anger I carry around, to listen to her scream all the horrible things I deserve to hear.

She only looks at me sadly. Remorsefully.

We stare at each other. Something in my chest aches.

"Good luck with your homework," she finally says, softly closing the door on her way out.

I wonder if I would have enjoyed that bike ride more if I'd have known it was my last.

ANSWERS

It's *nighttime again*, and I'm not sure what to expect as I crawl into my bed. I stay in my clothes, just in case. Part of me feels ridiculous about it.

I wake up the next morning. Nothing's happened.

Still, I'm so jarred by those two strange dreams that I continue to go to bed in my clothes.

Deep inside me, cobwebs have been shaken off something that I've buried down since childhood: a strange combination of fear and wonder, unrestrained by what most would call reality.

I can't ignore this feeling.

It's *not until one week later* that it happens again.

I wake up without any memory of falling asleep. This time, I'm alone in my bedroom — the Mysterious Girl is nowhere to be seen. But when I go to my window and look outside, I can see the oak tree sitting in the moonlit meadow.

I'm here.

I walk down the stairs. The occasional board groans beneath me. The entire interior of the house is cast in a strange lighting that gives everything a navy hue.

Instead of the back door, I head to the front door this time. I creak it open and peer outside. Much to my surprise, there's a small cobblestone road that leads from the door, down the hill, to what must be the smallest townsite I've ever seen.

It's barely the size of a small neighbourhood. The houses have an old French style to them, made of stone and wood. I can see signs of life milling about — people sitting on their porches, smoking, and walking down the streets. They don't seem to be paying much attention to me. *Townspeople.*

I wander down the road and into the town, keeping my eyes open for the Mysterious Girl. *She must be here somewhere. Maybe she can even give me a tour of the town.*

I lose myself in the cobblestone streets as I wander deeper and deeper into its heart. The town seems to be getting bigger as I go, expanding out before me. I'm passing by a dusty old alley when something unusual catches my eye.

A shadowy figure standing motionless in the middle of the alley, about twenty feet away. This person is different from the townspeople — while the townspeople barely look at me, the figure is staring right through me. I can't see the eyes, but I can tell.

It's just the two of us, alone together. For some reason, I feel an inexplicable urge to begin walking down the alley, but I plant my feet to the ground.

His outline seems to fade into the shadows around him, making him hard to decipher. When I look closer, though, I can make out little details. The figure looks like a small person who was stretched upwards like putty. The legs are like toothpicks poking out from a pair of black shorts that hang off the body. The arms are equally as thin — they slope inwards up to the bump of the elbow bone, which is their widest part. He really is nothing but skin and bones.

Ed.

My heart is pumping, a sickening sense of adrenaline intoxicating my bloodstream.

He's waiting for me. There's something eerily expectant in the way he stands so perfectly still.

Though I don't understand why, I want to get closer to him — some primal instinct.

Who am I, Ed, if not your faithful friend?

"Hey!" an energetic female voice calls out. I turn around, and the Mysterious Girl is striding towards me with a grin on her face.

When I look back down the alleyway, it's empty.

"I came back," I say, stating it as much to myself as to her.

The Mysterious Girl scans the area with her eyes. Did she see Ed? Or was it only me?

Where did he go?

"The Deep can be a dangerous place. Follow me," she says. She guides me into the darkened doorway of a nearby house.

The inside of the house is nearly pitch black, with scarce moonlight glinting off the edges of objects. When my eyes adjust, though, I can make out the shape of the Mysterious Girl wading through the darkness.

"I think I should tell you more about this place if you're going to stay." She pauses, a thoughtful expression on her face. "Well, I guess you don't really have a choice about whether you get to stay or not."

Dread in the pit of my stomach. *Am I trapped?*

She starts moving again. I follow.

There's no one in the house, but it still has signs of

life. It's as if the people living here simply disappeared into thin air.

We climb a flight of stairs, then up a rickety ladder into an old, empty attic. It smells like dry wood. At the far end of the attic, a small circular window.

"Over here," the Mysterious Girl instructs, crawling against it. I shuffle along on my hands and knees, crouch down beside her. She gazes outside. Small lights flicker inside the windows of some of the houses like little nestled stars.

"Ed won't find us here, will he?" I ask.

The Mysterious Girl shakes her head.

The way we're enclosed in the darkness, tucked away from the rest of this strange place — there's something comforting about it.

"Tell me about Ed," I say.

"Of course," she answers. "Ed . . . he has a power of sorts."

"A power?"

"Sometimes, it's going to feel like no one cares . . . But that's really not the case. They just don't see your suffering," she says, after searching for words.

"What do you mean?"

"Charlotte, you and I are the only ones who can see Ed," she explains softly. "It's a little trick of his. He's invisible to everyone else."

Silence as that settles in.

Her eyes are big and empathetic. "The longer you're in the Deep, the more you'll understand. About Ed, about me, about yourself . . . about everything." She tucks a loose strand of hair behind her ear. Wind whispers around the frame of this house. After a moment, she adds, "One other thing I can tell you about Ed is that he can morph and disguise himself into anyone."

"What?" A headache climbs my neck.

"He can change his appearance to look like people you know. People you care about." she says. "People are going to say things that hurt you. You just have to remember it's not them talking, they don't mean to cause any harm. It's Ed, trying to find a way to get to you."

I rub my eyes. "Now I have to decide whether someone I love is taking a shot at me or if it's Ed in disguise."

The wind whooshes outside.

"I'm sorry, Charlotte," the Mysterious Girl says solemnly.

I put my head against the window. The glass cold on my skin. I've begun to shiver.

The Mysterious Girl touches her forehead to the glass too. "Time works differently here," she states. "It moves much slower than in the waking world. It'll feel like you're here for an hour, tops, but the entire night will pass by."

I look down to the town below. Somewhere, Ed is stalking the streets. *Am I safe?* I'm not sure if I like it here, but from the little that I know, I can't escape. Every week, I'll keep coming back. And Ed will find me. It's beyond my control.

"What about you, then?" I ask. "What's your story? What do you want from me?"

"I'm here for my reasons," she says. "The real question is, what do *you* want from *me*?" She reaches into one of her pockets and pulls out a scratched gold pocket watch.

She flicks it open and stares down at its face.

Its rhythmic sound fills the air. *Tick. Tick. Tick.*

"Time's up," she says.

I *open my eyes*, and I'm staring at my bedroom ceiling. Beside me, a staticky radio song plays out of my clock. I put a hand to the side of my head. I can almost still feel the cold glass of the window.

THIS COLD STRUCTURE

A *couple of days later,* I'm curled up on the couch in front of the TV, trying to conserve body heat. The bus that was supposed to take me home from school was twenty-five minutes late — of course it had to happen on the coldest day of the month yet. That just about sums up my luck. I sat at the bench with Olivia as the autumn wind, icy with the promise of winter, whipped through my hair, around my body, through my bones.

"Are you okay? You look chilly," Olivia had said.

"I'm fine," I lied. "The bus will be here any second now, right?"

Now, the cold has cemented inside me; winter has made itself a house out of my bones. Not even the warmth of the indoors will make it go away. Fingers and toes — numb. Stinging in my hollow cheeks, teeth grinding. Frozen, bitter throbbing throughout my torso. My body shivers beneath a thin, decorative blanket.

Soft footsteps pad across the hardwood floor towards me.

"Your lips are blue," Parker says, leaning in for a closer examination.

"It's a bit nippy out there," I whisper.

He frowns. Chews his lip until I see a droplet of blood surface. Licks it away. "No, seriously. It looks like you ate a bunch of blue raspberry lollipops. Do you want me to get Mom or Dad?"

I shake my head. *What would they do, anyway?* "I'll warm up soon, it's alright."

After a pause, he says, "I'll be right back." He turns and runs upstairs, feet thumping loudly.

I soothingly trace my ribs with an icy finger. *You're okay. You're okay.*

Parker returns with a pile of blankets so big he can barely see over it.

"Damn, you're not messing around," I say, a half-hearted smile upturning the corners of my mouth.

"These are all my warmest," he says, carefully layering them on top of me. Faux fur is soft against my skin. He tucks the blankets around my shoulders, pulls them up to my chin. I'm engulfed in his scent — the soft forest smell, apples and greens, of Old Spice. Like a hug.

The shivering fades away as my muscles thaw. Heat — sweet, precious heat — slowly crawls back into my body.

"Better?" Parker asks. A detached ache in his eyes — a deep ocean, with no land in sight.

"Yeah."

He wanders over to the coffee table, where his manga resides.

"Thanks, Parker. I appreciate it," I say.

"No problem." He picks up the book and plops down onto the cushion next to me. "Let me know if you need anything." A sad smile on his raw lips.

I close my eyes.

My body stirs to life again — feeling returning to my fingers and toes, heated blood seeping through my veins, muscles unclenching. I plunge into the warmth until sleep quiets my mind.

WAITING

"The timing really is awful," Michelle observes thoughtfully at one of our sessions. "You have an eating disorder during a global pandemic. Normally, as part of the healing process, you would reconnect with teenage life. But now, with all these restrictions, you're stuck in a tricky situation."

"Tell me about it." I sigh in agreement.

These are supposed to be the best years of my life, and what am I doing with it? I can't help but think of all the opportunities I might've unknowingly missed out on, all the life experiences I'm not having. My youth's been stolen from me. The pandemic — a horrible disruption in so many teenagers' lives. My life has certainly come screeching to a halt, and I'm left waiting.

Waiting for what?

Oh, well. At least there's Ed to keep me company.

"It just doesn't make sense," I say. "Nothing deeply traumatic has ever happened to me . . . How did I end up so fucked up?" I can't help but feel I've let my parents down. They've worked hard to give me the lifestyle our family leads, and I repay them by getting an eating disorder. *Thanks for all your hard work! Oh, and here's some pain and suffering to affect the lot of you!*

"You've got a life-threatening eating disorder. Is that not traumatic enough?" Michelle responds.

I shrug. It still doesn't answer my question. Why.

"I've worked with enough clients to know that it's

rarely just one thing that creates an eating disorder," Michelle says.

Through starvation, I'm hurting myself. Hurting yourself is hurting the people who love you.

And you know what makes me feel even worse? This knowledge still doesn't give me the incentive to stop. I can't stop. I don't think I ever will.

I nod into Michelle's earnest face, but I'm afraid. Ed comes first — before my friends, before my family, before myself. What kind of monster does that make me?

THE PUZZLE

I open my eyes in the Deep. I'm wandering outside in the dark streets. The sky an endless blot of black.

Everything is still. The Mysterious Girl must be around somewhere. *I'll run into signs of life eventually.* I walk down a deserted road, footsteps echoing into the night, turn a corner, and my heart jumps in my chest.

There's a park, lit up by the pale moonlight. An old play structure beside a rusted swing set. On the other side of the playground, a field of dead grass. One of the swings is creaking gently, as if someone has just jumped off it.

Not just any park—the one by my house, that Parker and I go to. The sweet, warm blanket of innocence that once covered it has been brushed aside.

I approach the swings, reach out and grip on to the creaking one, stopping its motion.

I look around; no one is here.

I sit down on it, begin to move, looking out over the field of dead grass. There's an empty cavity in my chest. I glance over at the vacant swing beside me.

I push the ground with the tip of my toe, and the swing creaks back and forth. I'm numb.

Something catches my eye. The dead field. Little shapes, dark against the yellow of the grass. I slip off the swing and gingerly walk towards them.

Weird. Strewn puzzle pieces.

I get down on my knees and start collecting them.

I try to fit them together, but I can't seem to find any that will click.

Why are these here?

I sit down cross-legged and work away. The puzzle pieces are so dark they appear black, but the longer I stare at them, the more I begin to see faint traces of colour — navy blue, bruise puce, deep green. Damp, some bitten at the edges by mould. An instinctive knowing that I have to finish the puzzle. Now. Have to find out what picture it shows, what it all means.

I run out of time before I'm able to finish it, but the next time I'm in the Deep, I return. Soon, though, my curiosity burns into frustration. None of the puzzle pieces fit, no matter how hard I try.

The third night, my frustration churns into desperation. The chilling black sky hangs above me. Tears burn the corners of my eyes; I wipe at them hastily. Though I don't know why, something inside of me knows this is important. I stare at all the pieces, scattered out in front of me.

"A puzzle, I see?" a raspy male voice says softly. I look up. No one. Ed's presence. The air is colder.

Silently, I nod. My teary eyes return to the puzzle pieces. The wind brushes against my neck. Or is it Ed's hand?

"You've been working at that for quite some time now," Ed observes. He's right. I feel I've been desperately working on this puzzle long before finding this park. Weeks? Months? My entire life?

"And still, you've made no progress." Ed's tone isn't accusatory, only matter of fact. "Why is that?" The faint copper smell of blood.

Even though I want to deny it, I've known the answer for a while. The horror of the truth.

"It's impossible," I say quietly. "The pieces aren't made to fit together."

MAYBE

Sometimes, when Ed gets especially loud — especially violent — I read the old letters you wrote me years ago. I take them out of the box in my closet and store them away in my mind. I know they're old; irrelevant, one could argue. But, I don't know — there's something comforting in them. Maybe, between the handwritten lines, are faint whispers that there's something out there worth holding on for.

I know it's over. I know it's in the past. Still, it's a reminder that someone was able to get close to me — who wasn't Ed. Maybe something like that will happen again. Unlikely, I know, but maybe.

Maybe, if I squint at the horizon line, there's some distant chance that someone I haven't met yet could love me so completely and unconditionally.

Hope is rare, a sacred thing; you have to find it wherever you can.

Maybe.

Maybe.

Maybe.

CHAOS

Some people would burn a house to live in chaos.

I pray I'm not one of them; I pray I haven't led myself to this place out of an unalterable tendency towards self-destruction.

fear

/'fir/

noun

1. an unpleasant emotion caused by the belief that someone or something is dangerous, likely to cause pain, or a threat.

BREAKFAST

Another stark, overcast day. I'm wandering aimlessly up and down the school field, watching a frisbee fly through the air. The grass beneath my feet is dry and yellow. Around me, students move across the field — some running, some walking — as we play ultimate frisbee in phys ed. The cold morning air occasionally fills with a half-hearted cheer. Our team is lacking any form of team spirit whatsoever.

"Ugh, I'm so hungry," a girl groans.

"Why? Did you not have breakfast?" another girl asks.

"I don't usually have breakfast," the first girl says.

I wish there was a way I could turn my ears off. Ed is listening attentively. *Why does he have to be so competitive?*

"I *never* have breakfast," a third girl chimes in. I recognize the voice — it's Mara.

I clench my jaw.

"Breakfast is so overrated," Mara declares.

A dark shadow squeezes the inside of my chest as a couple other girls agree with Mara; I feel an isolating kind of remorse for every breakfast that I've ever shoved down my throat. *How could I be so gluttonous?*

I can't take this. I jog over to Mrs. Wright, who is standing by the side of the field, sometimes shouting at people to put in some effort. There's a sizable gap between her thin thighs, broadcasted to the world by tight black leggings. A red windbreaker with the school logo on the chest is draped over her narrow shoulders. She spots a group of girls standing around, chatting instead of play-ing, and calls, "Come on, girls! Let's get those summer bodies!"

Asshole. If I were a healthy weight, I could probably throw this woman like a javelin.

Her eyes settle on me as I approach. "What's up, Char-lotte?" Her voice is somewhat hoarse from all the yelling.

"Can I go to the washroom?" Anything to get away from the poisonous conversation happening amongst the girls.

"Sure," she answers. "Make it quick." With that, she turns, already shouting at the field again. I slink away through an opening in the fence that surrounds the field. After slipping a mask over my face, I pull open a heavy blue door to get inside the school. We don't have to wear masks outside, but the second we go back indoors, they come back on.

School. A battleground of words. Who can prove them-selves acceptable, the most attractive? Girls will try to do so by any means necessary.

I'll camp out in the bathroom for as long as I can with-out appearing suspicious.

Only, to my surprise, I'm not the only one here.

Two girls are sitting on the far side, backs against the wall. I don't recognize either of them. The first one, with dark, glossy black hair, has her chin in the air, her head resting back against the wall. Her closed eyes are squeezed shut and her forehead is wrinkled, giving her face a pained expression. The girl beside her has bright pink hair, but despite the confidence booming from her bold hair, her eyes are blank and unreadable.

It doesn't take me long to realize I've walked in on something. I avert my eyes and make a beeline for the nearest stall. Close the door behind me and stand there.

"I just don't know what's going on," a voice says. It sounds low, flat, soft, and has a slight quiver to it. I assume it must belong to the distressed girl. "I had one scrambled egg for breakfast, and I feel so guilty about it."

Oh no. Is there really no way to escape this?

"And then yesterday, I totally starved myself again," she continues. Her voice is strained now. "And my brother, who doesn't know — he's clueless — asked me if I was hungry."

I examine the dirt on my shoes, and the marks on the old red tiles beneath them. This conversation will trigger me, but I can't tear myself away.

"And I just started crying." The delicate voice breaks. Her sobs are quiet and airy, vulnerable gasps between the words she speaks. "Because of course I was, but *fuck.* I can't handle that shame."

She's right — the hellish, crushing shame isn't worth a temporary pause to the hunger, is it?

I have to get out of here.

I flush the toilet and burst from the stall, striding to the exit as quickly as possible. I head back to the field, where the conversation has thankfully moved on.

Part of me feels motivated to stop eating altogether after hearing that — '*if she can do it, why can't you?*' Ed says loudly.

The teary words of that girl haunt me — that voice comes from lived experience. It's authentic.

It's only going to get worse for her.

THE GIRL WITH THE BUTTERFLY TANK TOP

At *school,* my backpack drags down on my shoulders. My back aches from the weight.

The bell rang about ten minutes ago, and having just gathered my books from my locker, I step out the front doors. Another lonely grey autumn afternoon. The air feels heavy, as though rain is on the way.

I'm planning to meet up with Olivia on the front lawn — we'll take city transit home together from there.

I spot Olivia leaning against the side of the school. Something's wrong.

She's hunched over her phone, hair hanging in front of her face. Beneath the dark brown strands, her eyebrows are scrunched together.

I jog up to her, and she looks up. Her eyes are rimmed with faint red.

"What's wrong?" I ask, frowning.

She nods across the lawn at two girls wearing Brandy Melville — thin torsos beneath tank tops, one with an orange butterfly across the chest. They're huddled together. The butterfly girl leans in to whisper something in the other's ear; they giggle — stare straight at us.

"What's their problem?" I mutter.

Olivia's eyes are glued to the lock screen of her phone. "I went to elementary school with them."

"Oh." When she was younger, Olivia went to an apathetic private school, teeming with bullies. When her acne was acting up, they would leave takeout pizza menus on her desk. Whispering until she approached — then silence. For her birthday, her cousin gave her rainbow shoelaces; the next week, someone went after them with scissors. She ended up switching into the public system for junior high, where we eventually met in Grade 9 — it was a fresh start for her.

How could someone disrespect a person as compassionate as her?

"What are they doing here? Shouldn't they still be in the private system?" I ask. Prickly sensations in my fists.

"That school only went from kindergarten to Grade 9," she mumbles. She glances up at the girls, then back down at her phone. A haunted haze in her eyes.

"I'll fight them, Olivia, I swear to god," I say. I'm not very strong, but I bet I'd be able to muster the strength to break the butterfly girl's dainty, upturned nose. Crimson blood dripping down onto that god-awful print.

"Fuck them," she whispers. "Let's just get out of here."

"Fuck 'em," I agree. I make eye contact with the butterfly girl; she stops giggling and stares at me coldly, the corners of her lips upturning into a smirk. I stare back.

"Have they bothered you before?" I ask, glaring over my shoulder as we rush off the school campus. We head to the bus stop around the corner, safely out of sight from their cruel eyes.

Part of the Olivia I know seems to have returned as we distance ourselves from them.

Not all.

"This school," she sighs, shaking her head, not answering my question. "All this hype to get into Western. For what? To be reunited with a bunch of assholes? The ones who terrorized me throughout elementary?"

We join a small crowd of fellow students hovering by the bus stop bench.

"So you don't like it here?" Western — one of the highest ranking schools in the city, with all the confidence of an academic castle, looking over 17th Ave. There's literally green ivy climbing up the side of the building.

"I'm starting to think maybe I don't."

What would I do if she left?

We meet up before school, have lunch together, trek around 17th after school. Study in the library, loiter in the adjacent Shoppers Drug Mart, root around the nearby Mona Lisa art store. Anything is fun with her.

Who else would I hang out with? Mara, with her triggering commentary on food? Jade, always with Ana's malicious presence lurking nearby? I've drifted away from all the people I knew in junior high.

I look at Olivia. I *need you here.*

"Ah, here it is," she says as the bus rounds the corner.

We get in line and hop on, leaving Western's expansive brick facade behind us.

An unnerving glance into a part of Olivia's life I rarely saw.

Her past, returning with its hostile figures, taunting stares, sniggering voices.

Was it like that for her all the time?

THE LOSING GAME

My footsteps echo through the streets of the Deep.

The Deep is an interesting place. There's always something stirring beneath its pale moon, skipping through the meadow, crawling amongst the shadows of the streets. Tonight, I figure I'll just keep walking until I find something — or until something finds me.

I wander around a corner. One of the old-fashioned streetlamps up ahead has died, and there's a dark void of space between the streetlamp before and after it. Something's moving in the darkness though, shifting so calmly and gracefully it might as well be a part of it.

I stop walking and squint ahead of me. My eyes land on two eyes, shining through the dark. They're eyes that look like they could swallow up all the light in the world, and cast everything into peaceful darkness — the kind of darkness in your room before you fall asleep.

A voice whispers from the darkness, "Let's play a game."

It's the voice that's been keeping me company all this time, whispering things to me while I'm awake, trying to meet me in my dreams.

Ed.

When did you first crawl into my mind, intoxicating, addictive parasite that you are? Or have you been with me since the very beginning, waiting until I was at my weakest to strike?

"I'm not supposed to talk to you," I say quietly. My parents wouldn't want me to, and neither would Michelle. But for once, just once, can I do something I want to do?

"Come on," Ed presses gently. "Come play with me."

"People keep saying you'll hurt me," I answer, trying to stand my ground, but I can already feel myself crumbling away.

Ed ignores this. "I'm so lonely, locked up in this deep crevice of your mind. Do you feel lonely sometimes?"

"I do," I whisper, thinking even now how isolated and detached I feel from the real world. "Quite a bit."

"Well, that's one thing we have in common. Would you like to be lonely together?" he asks. There's a warmth in Ed's voice.

"I guess we wouldn't really be lonely then, would we?" I say.

"Exactly. Now, do you want to play a game?" he repeats.

"Okay."

I can sense him smiling through the darkness. It feels good, making someone happy.

"Here are the rules," he explains. "You lose as much weight as you can. Keep doing what you've been doing these past months — but be sneaky about it. You can't cause people reason for alarm. Ditch your snacks. Don't take much lunch. But they can't know — the only time they'll suspect something is when they see the number on the scale go down."

I furrow my brow. I know I shouldn't play. But the idea of losing weight sure does make it seem appealing. "Are you sure?" I say hesitantly.

"Yes, we like games, don't we?"

"We do. But what do I get if I win?"

Ed's eyes light up with eagerness. "A surge of euphoria at knowing you're in control."

I *wake up in my bed*, cold. I realize I've kicked all the blankets off onto the floor. I never got to answer Ed; I ran out of time.

Maybe I didn't need to answer.

Maybe I already know what I'm going to do.

EDMONTON

My parents and I fall into a new routine.

My part of the routine involves lying. I tell my parents that I put peanut butter and chia seeds into my smoothie when in reality I barely put in anything other than a couple meagre pieces of fruit. I'm supposed to have a morning snack; I lie about buying Starbucks. At least our family bank account is thanking me. Lunch is an easy win — since I'm at school, I'm not supervised. Since I don't have to be supervised, I'm able to get away with nibbling on a small muffin. I'm also supposed to have an afternoon snack; easy to skip. No one notices if a granola bar gets returned to the pantry.

I play Ed's game diligently.

Then we all sit down to eat dinner together. My parents both intently watch me eat. It's the hardest part of the day; there's no avoiding it.

I've counted all the calories. I shouldn't be gaining any weight at this rate. Still, I can't help but feel anxious. *What if I've miscalculated something? What will Ed say?*

I'm only caught once — by Parker. I close the pantry door after discretely chucking a granola bar back on to the shelf, and there he is, right beside me.

I jump. "Jesus, Parker," I say, waiting for my heart rate to calm down. "Don't sneak up on me like that."

His eyebrows are knitted together. "What are you doing?"

"What do you mean?"

He points to the pantry door. "Your snack. You put it back."

I pause. "A single granola bar isn't gonna make a difference," I say.

Deep eyes, full of worry. His voice is skeptical — "Is it just a single granola bar, though?"

Fuck. "Don't worry about it."

He sighs, an uncomfortable mix of exasperation and anxiousness. "This is gonna backfire on us," he says. "It's gonna backfire so bad."

I stare at him blankly. "Don't tell Mom." My voice comes out harsher than I anticipated.

"If you eat it, I won't have to." He scratches the back of his neck, shifting his weight from foot to foot.

"We're a team, remember? We help each other out."

"I don't see how letting you skip snacks is helping anyone," he says. I can see the conflict on his face.

"Come on," I beg. "Don't snitch on me. Don't do this."

"Eat it, just this once. Please." He looks just as desperate as I feel.

A pang in my chest. *Only for you, Parker.*

"Fine. Whatever." I snatch the granola bar back from the pantry and sprint upstairs. In the quiet of my room, I choke it down — slow, resentful nibbling. I pause periodically to wipe my teary eyes.

I see the referral sitting on the kitchen counter on a Friday afternoon.

It takes me a moment to realize what it is. I pick up the strange paper for further inspection.

What? My eyes fly over the next sentences. I'm gripping onto the paper too tightly, the edges crumpling beneath the pressure.

EATING DISORDER PROGRAM APPLICATION

This can't be for real.

> PATIENT: Charlotte Bellows
> SEX: F
> AGE: 15

My messy, disordered existence, summed up in the form of my name on this piece of paper. *What the hell is this?*

Heart pounding, stomach churning.

Sweat gleams in the creases of my palms.

There's no way to unsee this.

Edmonton? This is what my parents are planning? Ship me off to some hospital in another city?

The paper shakes in my hands.

I've damn well ended up like this because of them.

My face is burning hot.

"You're just gonna *fuck up* your child, and then send her away so a hospital can do the dirty work of fixing her?" I mutter, my voice shaking.

When Mom gets home, I wave the paper in her face. "Explain yourself!" I demand, voice rough. I hear my blood pulsing through me. My jaw is clenched.

Teetering on the edge.

She's in the kitchen, peeling potatoes for dinner.

Giant heaps of carbs. "If your father and I felt there was another way, we'd choose an alternative. But there isn't."

So Dad's in on this, too. Body-shame strangers one week, condemn your daughter to an eating disorder ward the next. *Ignorant accomplice.*

"Look at your vitals! You're *dying*, Charlotte! We've been trying at home, we really have been, but you're still nowhere close to where you need to be!" The whites of her eyes are turning red with tears.

White light rushes at me, through me. All the rage I felt first seeing the referral comes rushing back. My body tenses. Heat surges through me, starting at my face, coursing through my veins towards my hands. "You can't do this to me!" My voice pierces the air and fractures the space between us.

Mom takes a deep breath. Her voice is low and shaky when she speaks. "Can't you see, Charlotte? It's all we *can* do. We've booked an assessment at the hospital. In a couple months, we're going to drive up to Edmonton for it. Your father and I were going to try to tell you in a better way, but . . ." Her words peter out.

The hospital. It will be the end of everything. All my hard work, all my suffering to get to this size. For nothing. This huge change in my life — and my parents didn't even think to consult me. I will never let them do this to me!

"It's because we care," my mom adds.

Bullshit. If they cared, they'd have talked to me. They wouldn't have gone off and planned assessments behind my back. They would have just stopped *for once* and thought about how much this would hurt me. How much it *is* hurting me.

I *push past Mom*, storm upstairs, and slam my bedroom door behind me.

After moments — knocking, but I ignore it.

Tears streaming down my face, I stumble to my mirror and pull off my shirt. My entire body is trembling. I stare at my ribs — all twenty-four of them. Their definitive edges, the way they make bumps down my torso. They're still there. They haven't failed me.

I put my finger and thumb around my wrist. They can still touch.

My work is still evident.

I'm still here.

I'm okay.

For now.

But for now isn't forever.

JADE

I *stand there* in my bedroom for a while.

Eventually, Mom's footsteps tap away.

I stand a little longer.

Finally, I fall onto my bed, stare at my ceiling.

My anger simmers down into fear. They're going to do it — my parents are really going to ship me off to Edmonton. There's nothing I can do to stop them. All of this, completely out of my control. Hopelessness forms a crater deep in my chest.

Who would I even talk to about this? Most of the people I talk to wouldn't understand. They've complimented my 'model legs.' They've said, with good intent, that they wish they were 'Charlotte skinny.'

How fucked up is that? People see dying and mistake it for beauty.

I've never had the courage to tell them everything that's going on under the surface. Mostly because I know they won't have anything to say — it's something so far beyond what they're capable of relating to.

There's Olivia — I'd trust her with anything. But she's the one normal, teenage part of my life; I don't want to pollute that friendship with this.

A series of old memories come flitting through my mind.

Cold winter nights, fingers intertwined.

She would understand.

The bench.

Wouldn't that be a strange thing to do, though? To go back to something that caused past grief in order to sooth current grief?

It's the only option I can think of, though. I'm grateful to have it instead of nothing.

To talk about her though, we have to go way back. Way back to the start of my adolescence. And that girl named Jade.

Jade — her name still stirs up old emotion in me.

There was a different girl, first — her name was Ana. Throughout all of elementary school, we were best friends; everything we did, we did together. During recess, we'd come up with story ideas — I'd write them, and she'd draw the pictures for them. She was uproariously funny and creative, and always had my back. Year after year, she'd choose to play with me before anyone else. I really thought we would be friends for life.

Then, we went to junior high, and Jade entered the picture. Ana, Jade, and I all became friends. Things were different with Jade, though.

I remember when we first saw each other, more than friends, in the summer — something felt different.

Something felt perfect.

It was a warm September afternoon, in a field near the school. We lay there together in the lush grass, staring at the blue sky and watching clouds pass, talking and laughing. She plucked a dandelion from the ground and gently blew it. The seeds took flight, lazily gliding through the air. The sun bathed her in golden light. She glowed.

In class, later that week, I looked up to see her staring at me from the other side of the classroom. Her eyes nervously darted down to her papers; I smiled.

Crisp autumn air, fallen leaves underfoot. The wide and innocent eyes of a child in the mirror – unprepared but adventurous.

Eager smiles; beauty in simplicity.

She was the first girl I realized I had a crush on, the first person I came out to, and the first I dated.

"Are things going to be different at school?" Jade asked nervously, shortly after we'd confessed our feelings to each other. "Weird, I mean?"

I knew what she was hinting at – our friendship with Ana. What were we going to do?

"Not if we don't tell Ana," I finally said. I was so happy with our friend trio; if Ana knew of the connection between Jade and me, surely she would feel left out. I winced at the potential drama our relationship would cause. Also, *it's not like you can control who you fall for*, I reminded myself. I turned to Jade. "Do you think that's okay?"

She nodded. And so, we never told Ana – it was a sacred secret between Jade and me.

Talking to Jade had to be one of my favourite things. Her soft voice bloomed with care and warmth. The gentle vibration of my phone when she texted me – a reminder she was there and cared – always made me smile. The way she spoke to me, looked at me – she made me feel beautiful.

Her favourite shape was a triangle – the conviction and certainty in its angles. She liked the peacefulness of the rain — the fresh, sweet smell, the sound of it against the roof of her dad's car on a long drive. She would laugh when the wind blew her hair in her face and slide off one of the hair ties that were always around her wrists. When it was sunny, she closed her eyes and raised her chin, smiling serenely, basking in the warm light.

You were a new colour. I'd never seen anything quite like you before. And now, now that I've been exposed to this new vibrant hue, I see it everywhere. I've become colour-blind to everything else.

We were cold winter nights, soft fingers intertwined. An unbeatable closeness — real, deep, raw.

On blizzarding December nights, we nestled in my basement and watched horror movies, holding hands. She stroked my thumb with hers. I tried my best to make her feel cared for. I tried my best to make everyone feel cared for, but Jade especially.

Some days, Ana was trapped in a bad mood. One morning, she announced to me with an oddly boisterous pride in her voice that she had been diagnosed with depression. A strange gleam in her eyes, as though she was daring me to challenge her.

"I skipped breakfast today again," she announced to me another morning. "I probably have an eating disorder or something."

She scratched at the backs of her hands until her skin broke, then promptly showed it to Jade and me. *Is this a cry for help?*

That night, I texted her mom. *Better to let her know before things get out of control.* She thanked me for informing her and told me she was glad Ana had a friend like me.

While Ana shared everything, Jade was much the opposite. She didn't like to talk about her past, and only when I looked back did I realize unusual things about her — blank expressions that fell over her face, strange things she would say, bizarre rituals she would repeat in her everyday life. They made no sense.

"You know what's so special about you?" she told me one night. "You care without knowing the end result." I still wonder what she meant.

I spent lots of time worrying about Jade, the last thing she probably wanted, but you can't control caring, can you? I wanted to help, but what could a thirteen-year-old do?

I tried. I tried to help this mystery that was Jade.

I suspect something happened in her childhood. There was never any clarity, though — all I could do was grasp fleeting possibilities. I think she wanted it that way. So, in the end, that's how it was left —

A mystery.

When we're younger, we believe anything is possible. We believe we can save anyone.

She wanted a girlfriend, she told me, not a therapist. Helping people was in my nature. I didn't understand how someone wouldn't want to be helped.

You're like a sad song — it hurts to listen to you, but you're so beautiful. Maybe it's your lyrics. Maybe it's your melody. Maybe it's something else entirely. Whatever it is, I don't think I'll ever get tired of it. So, I put you on repeat.

Again.

Again.

Again.

I sat with her on the bench in the greenspace, two years ago. Both of us staring at the ground in front of us, scalding tears. She handed me a travel-sized package of tissues.

I still think of her when I pass by that bench — where everything changed. It *will never be the same.*

Things were different without her.

Something beautiful, shattering into painful, unfixable shards.

I took down our pictures, put away our letters. It all went into a shoebox that resides in my closet. I held her hoodie, which smelled like her, and felt like her. Some mystifying urge to keep it — reluctant to give it back.

We didn't text. We didn't talk anymore, either. At school, we barely looked each other's way. I kept trying to believe she wasn't the same person that remained perfect in my memory, unfractured by time. I knew my version of Jade was in her somewhere, still.

I wanted her laugh to light up the dark in my mind. I still felt it, the warmth of her laugh. It would pass through the boundary of our new reality. Just a final reassurance that she was happy.

She disappeared from school for weeks at a time — strange, for someone who was so involved in her academics. When she did show up, and she thought no one was looking, she stared off into space vacantly.

And so, the girl with the prettiest smile didn't smile anymore.

This is when the whole thing accidentally slipped out to Ana.

What if she had never found out? Things would have been easier, that's for sure. Ana knew that Jade and I were having troubles, that we didn't hang out anymore, but up until now, she thought it was just friendship struggles.

Jade had been talking to her when she accidentally let it slip that we'd "broken up."

"'Broken up?' What do you mean?" Ana demanded.

Jade stared at her for a moment — there wasn't really any coming back from a statement like that. She texted me to reluctantly explain the situation:

I told Ana that we were in a relationship.
I'm sorry.

My phone exploded with text messages from Ana:

You and Jade dated??
What the hell??
For how long?

Shit.

This new information completely changed Ana — she quickly became bitter and malevolent. She stayed close to both of us, though, giving a manipulative facade of friendship. A difficult situation got even worse.

"How's your weekend going?" I asked Ana when I met up with her one Sunday.

"Better than Jade's," she answered. "Did you know she's got six guys trying to get with her on Snap? Six!" She shook her head in awestruck disbelief. "She's only interested in two of them, anyways."

Something in my chest ached. *She's already talking to new people?* "Have you made any new art?" I tried again.

"Ooo, yes! Let me show you!" she exclaimed, sliding out her phone. The conversation thankfully moved on.

A few weeks later, though, Ana had a new announcement: "Jade's got a *boyfriend!*"

"Oh."

There was a strange gleam in her eyes that I'm only now able to recognize as cruelty. "Did you know he's sixteen?" she asked with too much eagerness.

"Three years older?" My voice was quiet.

"Yeah. He's like six feet tall, with brown hair, and he's *so* handsome. I actually met him the other week, and he's quite the gentleman, too." Ana watched me closely for a reaction.

I looked away and tried to blink away the tears. I could feel myself beginning to crack, more and more every day, every time I had another goddamn conversation with Ana. Jade was all she talked about. Jade Jade Jade. But Ana was all I had; in some twisted way, since she was the only person I was out to other than Jade, she was the only person I felt really understood me. It would be many months until I met Olivia.

Then, she told me that she'd been telling Jade all the things I'd been confiding in her—"To make things fair," she said. No wonder things weren't going well when it came to healing with Jade—I'd trusted Ana to help me work through everything, and she'd betrayed me.

She even went as far as to call me a 'doormat.' "You let people walk all over you," she said, while doing so herself. Ana told me that Jade was saying horrible things behind my back, questioning why she ever dated me in the first place.

I never intentionally tried to hurt Ana. She, however, went out of her way to hurt me.

I sat with Ana on the dirty, scuffed hallway floor after school. I was bending over my papers, which were scattered across the floor as I feebly tried to organize them. She was leaning against her locker, doodling absentmindedly in a sketchbook she always carried around.

"I was talking to Jade today about you, you know," she said, trying to sound nonchalant. There was that strange undertone of pleasure in her voice, though.

I paused. *Not this. Not now.* It's not like there was any stopping her, though. When she wanted to talk about Jade, nothing I could say would quiet her. I took a deep breath and continued stacking my papers.

"We were talking about all the crop tops you've been wearing since the breakup."

I glanced down at myself. I was wearing one right now. After the breakup, Parker had insisted on the power of retail therapy. There was something empowering about embracing my body; I was starting to feel confident in my own skin.

Ana sighed. "You're so pretty. I don't know why you have to dress like that." She paused, focusing on her drawing for a moment, then asked, "Is it attention? Is that what it's for?"

"No," I answered flatly. *What am I supposed to say to that?*

"Well, Jade said you look like a slut," she said. She tossed those words out so casually, as if she was talking about a band or a class.

"Can we talk about something else, please?" I asked. I clipped a stack of papers into my binder. Pretended my hands weren't shaking as much as they were.

"I mean, at least you've got her jealous," Ana added.

"Jealous?" I repeated, looking up at her. "Over what?"

"Your body. She always comments about how thin your waist is. It's *paper thin* from a sideview. I mean, you've got hips, though. Very feminine build." She rested the eraser of her pencil against her lip for a second, examining her work with critical eyes. Her eyes briefly shifted towards me; she sized up my body with that same expression. "She says you're probably gonna be a model or something."

Before I could answer, she held up her sketchbook for me to see. "What do you think?"

It was a girl who had a striking resemblance to Jade. "It's good. Realistic," I said.

"Thanks," she said with a smile, looking me in the eyes for the first time in the conversation. For a brief moment, I thought I really saw her — my old childhood friend. But a cloud passed over her eyes. She returned to her drawing and continued speaking. "You know what else she said?" Taunting bitterness in her voice.

"My bus is gonna be here soon, I should really get going," I mumbled, gathering the last of my papers and standing up abruptly. *Please stop please stop please stop.* I opened my locker and pulled out my backpack, stuffing my papers inside.

"She said," Ana continued, ignoring me, "when you were kissing, you put her hand on your boob."

Heat rose to my cheeks. "What! That never happened!"

Why would she lie about something like that?

"It's okay, don't worry." She smirked. "I didn't believe her. It's not like you've got any boob for her to touch, anyways."

I bit the inside of my lip. *Don't cry don't cry don't cry.* She'd developed a strange fixation on the size of my chest, and always made sure I knew it. "I've gotta go," I whispered in a strained voice. This girl beside me was a completely different person — someone I wished I had never met.

"By the way, don't tell Jade I said that," Ana said. "She would kill me."

Maybe she should, Ana. Maybe she should. Not that I would ever have the courage, though. I closed my locker with more force than I intended and rushed down the hall.

"Have a nice night!" she called out behind me, still obliviously working at that stupid drawing.

The second the school door closed behind me, I broke out in convulsive sobs. Nose running, struggling to breathe through teary gasps.

Ana and Jade, the two people closest to me — gone.

I roughly wiped my eyes and tried to figure out where I had messed up so badly.

The sky was grey. The fluffy, white snow that used to blanket the ground had melted away to reveal dead grass.

Damp. Cold.

To this day, I still don't know if Jade really said those things or if it was just Ana making things up to hurt me. I've chosen to believe the latter.

Eventually, though, I'd had enough. I called Ana out over text.

> You haven't been treating me with the same respect as you usually do. Sometimes when we talk, I walk away feeling bad. We've been friends for a long time. I'm wondering — what's going on?

She'd turned it all around to make it seem like I was the problem:

> A couple people have tainted my view of our friendship and it's made me very scared lately. I constantly feel like you're going to leave me or hurt me really bad.

Right. I was the one who was going to hurt *her*. I once read that sometimes people will pretend you're a bad person so they don't feel guilty about the things they did to you. Though I already had a feeling I knew the answer, I asked,

> Who's this?

> Well, I was told by someone close to me that you're kind of a selfish person and you usually do things based on what you want, and then someone else important to me said the same thing.

So when I stopped being a 'doormat,' I was selfish.

It would only make sense for this to be coming from Jade. I didn't blame her, though — it had been a difficult breakup. I had my own hard feelings towards her, at the time; feeling bitter was less painful than feeling alone. *It's all part of the healing process, isn't it?*

Months later, Jade would text me:

I'm so sorry for ever hurting you.

Even if we didn't talk much anymore, we came to good terms. Ana, however, never gave me an apology. Just:

My mother originally brought it up.
That you're selfish, I mean. Then I
relayed it to Jade, and she agreed.

Shout out to Ana's mom, for being a forty-five-year-old woman going after a literal fourteen-year-old who was trying her best. Stay classy, Deborah.

So in the heat of it, when Jade and I needed space, Ana was the double agent who wouldn't give either of us a rest from the difficult situation that had settled between us. It shouldn't have been such a surprise that things got so bitter. Sometimes I wonder if how I felt during all of this even crossed Ana's mind. *Why would she manipulate me like that?*

Eventually, the two of them went off on their own. I became the outcast. During lunch break, I would glance over to see them hugging. Jade would put her head on Ana's shoulder, and Ana would have the smuggest expression on her face.

I'd lost control of the situation, and I'd completely lost control over how I felt.

Several months later, it was Grade 9, about halfway through the year. In a couple months, COVID-19 would begin rapidly spreading throughout Calgary, and we would go into lockdown, not that any of us could have predicted this.

I was at my locker at the end of the day, shoving papers and binders into my bag. The hallway was mostly empty already.

A timid tapping at my shoulder. I turned around. Jade was standing there, her backpack slung over her shoulder.

"Hey," I said.

"Do you want to walk home together?" she asked.

The day was wintery and brisk, but the sun still shone brightly. This time, Jade didn't close her eyes and raise her face to the light. Her eyes were focused on her boots, which crunched into the blindingly white snow as we ambled along.

"How've you been?" I asked.

She looked up at me, barely blinking. "I've been better, honestly," she admitted.

"Is it school?"

She shook her head, paused for a moment, and said, "I was discharged from the hospital a couple weeks ago."

"Oh." *That must be why she was missing so much school.* "I'm sorry." I never asked why. I'd overstepped those boundaries in our relationship, and it had ruined everything. I vowed to myself I was never going to do it again. So, instead: "Is it good to be back home? Or no?"

A silence — she was thinking. "I don't know." Her voice was genuine and pensive. She said, "I've fallen behind on so much schoolwork. I can't imagine what high school is going to be like."

"It's almost 2020. Maybe it'll be a good new year."

"Maybe." She sounded doubtful.

We walked together for a couple more blocks — making small talk about her cats, about Parker, about the weather — until reaching the intersection where she would cross to the other side of the road and disappear into her neighbourhood.

"Bye," I said, mustering a smile.

"Goodbye." She smiled back — something troubled in her eyes.

I trudged through the snow alone, through the still streets of my own neighbourhood. Past the bench where we had broken up all those months ago. Its wood was chipped; its metal arm rests tinged with rust.

Jade — alone in an unrecognizable place, with sick, unrecognizable people. The tears left my eyes warm but were already cold by the time they dripped from my chin.

Tonight, I text her:

> When you went to the hospital last year, were the people there nice? You don't have to answer, but it's not a random question if you know what I mean.

I put my phone down on my bed and shift my gaze back to the ceiling. When I hear my phone buzz, I quickly pick it up again.

The people were very nice, and you're all in the same boat together, so it's easy to connect. We played a lot of Uno.

Do you think you'll be put
in the hospital?

                                    Maybe. I'll find out on
                                    December 10th. But Uno
                                    does sound pretty fun.

You don't have to answer,
but what would it be for?

Psychology, the one class we have together, is in the
coldest room in the school. I never go inside without a
puffy winter jacket, and since I usually wear sweatpants,
there would be no opportunity for her to see what my
body really looks like.

　　I think about Ed and his milky eyes staring up at me
from the ground below my bedroom window. I start
typing, delete what I wrote. She texts again.

Are you okay?

I think about my twenty-four ribs and my wrists.

                                    In this moment, yes.

You can always call me
when you aren't.

That part of her hasn't changed, and I'm grateful for it.

RAZORS

That night, hours later, I lie very still in my bed and imagine myself dissipating into the air around me. Even if I can't see him, I know that Ed is lying next to me. He will never leave me alone.

I think something in my mind has been horribly stained.

Sometimes, my mind is a flurry of thoughts, each one shouting over the others in an attempt to be heard; it's absolute chaos, then. Today is different, though. It's quiet. It's bad when it gets loud, but it's worse when it gets quiet.

I could do it.

I could bleed away into the silence — still.

The sun has already set. I crawl out of my bed and walk to my bedroom window. My reflection stares back. Beyond that, the alleyway is still.

I look to the bathroom connected to my bedroom. The lights are turned out, but the bathtub shines through the darkness. A little bead of water falls into the sink.

Drip.

I trudge towards the bathroom. Silent step by silent step. I pick up a razor sitting on the bathtub's edge and stare at it. Like the bathtub, the blade is glowing.

In a sudden motion, I slam the razor head against the sink; the cheap plastic cracks instantly. I slide the blade out, lightly caressing it with my fingertips.

I'm not me anymore — this is Ed.

My god, get this parasite out of my mind.

A key . . . There must be a key to the lock of this door that holds me hostage, that isolates me from the rest of the world.

What is this key?

Where do I find it?

And a voice whispers, 'Maybe the key is in the shape of a razor blade. Maybe the light will shine through the open door as blood shines through your open wrists.'

I've thought about death.

Something strange inside me rebels against this — I don't want to die. Dying means you leave behind traces of emptiness.

A trail of memories and feelings no one knew but you.

Things you wanted to say but never had the chance to.

Empty desks, empty beds, empty chairs. Those places where you will never see someone again.

I don't want to inflict this pain on other people. I don't want to die, I just want to disappear. Here one second, gone the next, no emotional mark.

The concept of suicide is a complicated one.

There are consequences that have to be balanced — have you given more than you took from other people's lives? Would life be better without you?

I drop my head in my hands. I wish I could dismantle my brain, fix all the little broken pieces, and put it back together right.

Ed holds the razor blade very lightly against my left wrist, just tickling the surface of my skin. I don't believe that he has any intention of actually killing me — not in this moment, at least. In all truth, I don't even think he wants to scare me. No, Ed isn't quite like that. All he wants to show me is that between the two of us, we have control. The only ones with power over my death — Ed and me.

Ed has proven his point.

I put down the blade and go back to my bed.

When I next open my eyes, the oak tree is outside my window.

Every seven nights, it just keeps on coming back.

I sneak through my house. From somewhere inside its depths, I can hear the faint sound of a clock.

Tick. Tick. Tick.

I push upon the front door and slip outside into the cool night air. Down the cobblestone road, the little town looks just as it looked before. I head towards it.

Who am I looking for? The Mysterious Girl? Ed? Someone. Anyone.

I pass a grimy woman reclining on her porch chair, softly plucking a guitar. The melody melts into the night. I pass a nicely dressed man sitting on the curb, his head in his hands. He doesn't move as I walk by.

Then, he's there. That tall, narrow body standing in the middle of the road. His shadow, cast by the moonlight, even longer and thinner than he is. There's comfort in his familiarity.

Ed smiles lightly and waves to me with his bony, delicate fingers.

I wave back.

He turns around and begins walking, and I can tell he intends for me to follow. I start trailing him, trying to quicken my pace to catch up. I don't know where he's going, but I want to go there, too. The soft music wraps me in a warm, calm feeling as I go.

"Charlotte!" I turn around to see the Mysterious Girl dancing towards me from the other side of the street. When I glance over my shoulder, Ed is gone. *Damn it*, I think. *I've lost him again.*

It's okay, though, I remind myself. Ed will come back. He always does.

I turn my attention to the Mysterious Girl.

Crossing one leg in front of the other, she pushes off the tips of her toes and spins. In time to the music, she leaps elegantly into the air. There's something mystical about the way she moves.

"You do ballet?" I ask as she dances closer.

"We're in the Deep," she reminds me. "I can do anything I want." She nods in the direction of the meadow. "Come on. I've been waiting for you."

The Mysterious Girl, always on the move. She runs toward the meadow. Slips through the night, moving so smoothly yet swiftly, it's almost like she's floating.

I follow her all the way to the oak tree, where she sits down and leans against its sturdy trunk. She pats the ground beside her, inviting me to join her.

When I lean back against the tree, I have to shift around a while before I can get comfortable. The oak's bark is hard against my spine.

We look up for some time. Millions of stars glow from the purple and navy hues of the sky.

"I see you've had a tough day," she states.

"How did you know?" I ask, glancing over at her.

"I have a natural advantage in the Deep," she reminds me with a smile. "An insider's scoop, if you will."

The breeze curls around us. "Mom wants to send me to the hospital," I tell her.

"Wants?"

"Well, she's going to, anyways."

"You're scared."

"And mad."

She looks at me, head tilted. "Mad?"

"My parents think the hospital is some great solution. Just send her off, fatten her up, and move on in life." I dig fists into my eyes. "It's already so difficult, and if I went to the hospital, it would be even more difficult. I would be in an unknown city surrounded with a bunch of other sick people."

"That's true. It would probably be like summer camp, except nobody's happy and everyone looks like they had cocaine for breakfast," she adds.

"Well, that's a nice way of putting it." I roll my eyes.

The Mysterious Girl grins, then looks at me seriously again. "I'm living here with all your thoughts. I understand you," she assures me.

"My mom understands a little. I just wish she would understand more."

"No, you don't."

"What do you mean?"

"Her lack of full understanding is what is protecting her," she says. "There are just some paths we have to walk alone."

I can see her point. I've already caused so much struggle for my family. "Do you think my family would be better off without me?" Frigid loneliness shivers. Emptiness.

"They'd be devastated if you killed yourself," the Mysterious Girl says.

"I know." A single firefly floats from the grass like a fallen star. Disappears whence it came. "I just mean like if I never existed in the first place."

"I guess we'll never know."

Neither one of us says anything for several minutes. We listen to the crickets. The grasses around us, brushed by a subtle gust of breeze, bend before it. Maybe if I stare at her for long enough, something will finally click — an idea, a solution, an epiphany.

"Should I kill myself?" I ask the Mysterious Girl.

"Not yet," she answers simply.

The leaves of the oak tree rustle.

"One of these days it'll feel like I won't have a choice."

"That's possible," she says. "One day you might not have a choice. But today, Charlotte, you still do."

I search the sky for recognizable constellations. "I guess we're never not in danger of ourselves." I realize its truth as I say it.

The Mysterious Girl looks over at me, eyebrows knit. "I promise to protect you for as long as I can."

"What happens when you can't?"

She looks back to the sky, and stays silent for a very long time.

The entire universe hangs in the sky above us. It makes me feel so small. So lonely.

"I'd rather be a victim of Ed than a victim of reality," I say.

She answers grimly, "It looks like you might be a victim of both."

Is there any real purpose beyond Ed?

A strange thought comes to mind. "You said one of Ed's powers was that he could change his appearance."

The Mysterious Girl nods.

The thought builds in my mind like a snowball rolling down a hill, getting bigger, gaining momentum. "Oh dear god," I whisper. "Please tell me you're not Ed."

The Mysterious Girl doesn't look away from the sky. "Why are you so afraid of this possibility?" she asks me.

I feel the familiar sensation of the back of my eyes burning with tears, but quickly wipe them away. "Because sometimes it feels like you are all I have."

MILLIONS OF BROKEN LITTLE PIECES

Snow clings on to buildings, and my body burns with cold.

I know I'm getting closer to the end.

I'm sitting on my bed, staring out my bedroom window at an overcast sky. There's something about the cold, monotone grey of the clouds that pulls me up into them.

I'm free-falling, spiralling downwards.

Where's the meaning? Where's the purpose?

In my lap is a piece of paper resting on top of a hardcover book. My hand loosely grips a pencil, and I gently touch the lead to the paper in a consistent, rhythmic

Tap.

Tap.

Tap.

Words bleed from the pencil tip onto the paper. It takes me a moment to realize the gravity of the words I'm writing. I feel the presence of someone sitting beside me — Ed.

I write:

Like freezing to death, it hurts very much. At first.
Now it's just numb;
I'm sorry.
I tried.

I yank my hand away. Is that what this is? A suicide note? A desperate cry for help? Or simply the playscript to some sick fantasy?

I take the note and rip it up into millions of little pieces — millions of broken little pieces. Indecipherable to all.

Except you, Ed. You understand. Don't you?

I snatch up all the ripped pieces and glue them to a paper — a collage of unassuming suffering.

Why is suffering so beautiful? Why is beauty so painful?

I tack the collage up in my room. Pain disguised as art.

THE EYE

The tornado that is this mess continues to ravage my mind.

When I think of the future and don't see myself, I know just how bad Ed is for me. But when I think of the present, he's all I have. He'll know exactly what to say to comfort me. He always does. He's been patiently waiting for me to speak to him.

Tell me there's such thing as control. Tell me it's not the illusion I fear it is.

'*Are you even paying attention to me, Charlotte? Fear is control. Can you feel the eye of the storm? The calm in the midst of all this chaos?*'

I feel close.

'*You are. I'll take you to the eye of the storm. When you're there, you'll control the storm. It will be peaceful. Powerful. Beautiful.*'

What will I have to do to get there?

'*You must walk head-on into the storm.*'

I don't think I'll make it. I think this storm will kill me.

'*Who's to say death isn't the eye?*'

ALL THESE YEARS AND I STILL CAN'T UNDERSTAND YOUR INTENTIONS

I'm walking to the school's front doors one morning when I see Ana sitting on a bench on the front lawn with Jade. I can't help but stare at her as I walk by. She waves at me. We lock eyes. Am I staring at my childhood friend, or the girl who ridiculed me with insults?

How can she wave at me like that? How can she pretend she never treated me the way she did?

Anger sparks.

This isn't the first time I've felt this towards her. I have moments when I want to get in an aggressive confrontation with her, and moments when I want to sit down with her and just ask her why.

If I really look deep enough at her, I still see the little girl with the bright pink headband who approached me, smiling, on the first day of Grade 1, when I didn't know anyone yet. Is she the same person?

At that memory, though, I calm down a little.

I truly hope she doesn't treat Jade the way she treated me.

Despite all the hard feelings I have towards her, I wave back.

UNDONE

Olivia's Docs sit by the front door. Saturday night, I step around them and into the foyer, but not before noticing the laces of the left boot — at every spot where the lace crosses the tongue, it's cut, all the way from the toe to the top of the ankle. The laces gape like a cracked-open ribcage.

"What happened?" I ask, nodding to them as I kick off my shoes.

Olivia, patiently waiting for me, pauses. Faint, dark circles beneath her eyes — but on each far corner, a small rhinestone. "My dog got to them," she finally says, and smiles. "Come on, I've got cards set up in the basement!"

She turns and disappears into the house. I glance at the laces one last time — the preciseness, the sharpness of the lines.

The basement is dark. In the moment before Olivia turns on the lights, her rhinestones gleam delicately through the shadows like tears. A frown, an odd tension in her eyes.

With the flick of a switch, the strange, pained aura flicks off her face; light fills the room. The rhinestones return to their sparkly, artistic state.

I saw something there, though.

"Poker?" Olivia suggests when we sit down at a card table downstairs.

"Yeah!"

An idea lights up her eyes. "What if we bet peanut M&M's!"

"Sure," I say, knowing I'm not going to be able to eat them anyway. She runs off to get them.

While she's gone, her dog — a spotted mutt that resembles a chihuahua — scurries down the stairs, and sniffs around my feet. "Hello!" I bend down and pat his soft head. Dull, circular teeth peek out of his panting mouth.

You didn't do that to Olivia's laces, did you?

He stares up at me with blank, beady eyes.

No. Only scissors could do that. And someone with an opportunity.

"Paul!" Olivia exclaims. I look up to see her coming back down the stairs with a yellow package of the chocolates. She drops the M&M's off at the table and scoops her dog up in her arms. Paul nestles into her chest before she puts him back down and tears open a package.

"Here, these are yours," she says, sliding over twelve candies. I sort them into colours — red, orange, yellow, green, blue, dark brown. I imagine the smooth chocolate melting on my tongue, teeth crunching through the peanut centre.

I blink. *Don't do this to yourself.*

Paul wanders in a few inattentive circles before scuttling off.

Olivia deals out the cards.

"Wanna go to Michaels again sometime soon?" I ask. "We could get you some new laces — in a funky colour, even. White would be super cool."

"I'm pretty sure white shoelaces on Docs represent white supremacy."

"Okay, never mind then. A different colour. But what do you think?"

She nods. "It *has* been a while since we've gone to Michaels. I just don't know if there's much point in buying new ones." Pauses. "It's five cards in a poker hand, right?"

"Yeah, I think so," I say.

She slides me my hand, plops an M&M in her mouth.

The next time I see Olivia, the laces are completely gone. She's forced to trudge around like she's injured. We're walking through the school hallways between classes one Monday when we pass by one of the Brandy Melville girls. She glances down at Olivia's loose boot, and though half her face is covered by a mask, a leer poisons her eyes.

A churning feeling in my gut that something's going on — but how do I help Olivia if she doesn't tell me?

Off to Michaels — sitting side by side on the bus, an earbud in each ear. Her music is more subdued this time.

The store has a wall full of shoelaces, from earthy, industrial tones to bold neons. Olivia goes for black. There's nothing hopeful or excited in her eyes as she picks the new black shoelaces from the shelf — a quiet echo of dread.

"I'll cover it," I say in the checkout line.

"Are you sure?"

I smile. "Yeah, don't worry about it."

I wonder how long we'll have until these shoelaces get cut up, too.

THE CALGARY WARD

"Why Edmonton, though?" I ask Michelle one Tuesday afternoon after school. My first response of frantic panic has passed. It's been replaced with numb shock. Stun gun shock. I don't want to believe it. "Isn't there one in Calgary?" I don't want to go there, either, but at least I might be able to see my friends and family. In Edmonton, it would be like I'd be in a whole new, unknown world.

"The Calgary eating disorder ward has a reputation for being awful," Michelle explains. "The refeeding process there is fear based, not support based. They pretty much scare you into eating. Which doesn't really work, because you're already scared of eating in the first place. It leaves some girls with PTSD."

"How do they scare you into eating?"

"Well, they threaten to give you a feeding tube."

"Oh." A feeding tube. That would be horrible.

"In Edmonton, though, they try to work through the fear with you. They understand that recovering from an eating disorder is more than just gaining weight." Michelle takes a sip of the tea she has beside her. "There are patients from all over the country trying to get into Edmonton. We try to make sure all our clients go to Edmonton instead of here."

"Do I even have time to turn things around, though?" I ask her. The hospital seems inevitable. I could try. I feel Ed beside me. He murmurs, '*Don't commit!*'

"Well, your assessment in Edmonton is in three months. For most girls it's longer, but you're in such a dangerous state that they've let you come sooner," she answers. "And yes. Try to turn things around. What if you just gave in to Edmonton? You'd be going there for sure. You'd eliminate any chance you have of *not* going."

I close my eyes.

I don't think I can do this.

VITALS

Mom drums her thumbs against the steering wheel. Right thumb, left thumb, right thumb, left thumb; she keeps flipping from one radio station to the next, until I finally say, "This song is good, Mom," just to stop her fidgeting. Also, I've never seen her drive so carefully. We're going so slow that I feel bad for the drivers behind us.

"The speed limit's fifty," I remind her.

"I know," she says.

We crawl through the city streets, into the heart of downtown, towards the Sheldon Chumir Centre. It's time for my routine vitals checkup. To track progress. Ha. Progress. Just another word for getting fatter, which I've had no interest in actually doing. So we mostly just look at the vitals, say, "well, shit," and go home.

Mom turns off 12th Ave and drives into the underground parking lot. Cold concrete swallows up the sky as we go down, and stops the satellite radio from coming through. Static. Mom pulls into a parking stall and stops the car. She sits there for seconds before opening the door. *What is she thinking?*

"Let's go," she says, and steps out of the car.

The parkade smells like moist gas as we walk through it. Mom calls the elevator, and the doors open for us. She presses the button. Floor three. Hastily pays for parking on her phone while I watch the numbers on the cheap elevator screen above the doors go up. It smells faintly of cigarettes in here.

1 . . .

2 . . .

3 . . .

The doors open.

The Sheldon Chumir is my favourite hospital. It has grit. It has *character*. Because it's downtown, lots of drug addicts go there. As we walk through the room full of people waiting to get their bloodwork done, I make sure to get a good look at my surroundings.

Mom tells my name to a woman working in front of a big computer screen behind a counter, shows her my healthcare card, and we go to sit down. After taking a squirt of gooey hand sanitizer from a dispenser at the edge of the room, my fingers feel chilled and faintly sticky.

The masked people in the room are great for face tattoo idea inspiration. They're all pretty badass. One guy in his twenties has a teardrop on the side of his face, and a frowny face with Xs for eyes between his eyebrows. Fascinated, I stare at him until he looks at me, and then I quickly look away. I wonder what face tattoo I would get. *What about a backbone down the side of my face?*

"Charlotte?" a woman in a lab coat calls from the counter.

I stand up.

"Room twenty-four."

I walk past the counter and down a hallway with numbers painted above the doorways.

22 . . .

23 . . .

The room smells strongly of disinfectant.

I take a seat on an uncomfortable chair. After endless visits, I know the drill. It's just one long, step-by-step procedure. A woman comes in and burrows a needle deep into the inside of my elbow. I feel its sharp tip dig into me and stay there for a moment. I glance over to see a vial filling up with my velvety-red blood. My arm aches as she slides the needle out.

"Follow me," she says without turning, and leads me into a different room. A polyester bed with a long sheet of paper covering pulled over it, beside an EKG machine. That's all.

"Have you had an EKG test before?" she asks.

"Yeah." Every week.

"You know what to do, then." She passes me a piece of paper with two arm holes, leaves the room, and I pull off my shirt.

For a moment, I run my finger lightly over my torso, feeling the divots of the space between my ribs. I feel myself relax. Tossing my shirt to a chair in the corner of the room, I pull the paper top over my shoulders. The room is freezing. I shiver within the thin folds of the paper.

When she comes back, I lie down on the bed, and she attaches the gooey little stickers on my chest, arms, and ankles. They're icy against my skin.

Next, a cord attaches onto the stickers. I stay still for a couple minutes as she stares at the screen.

"All right, all done with the EKG," she finally declares, briskly unhooking the wires from the stickers on my skin. "I'll give you a moment to change."

When she leaves, I don't even bother pulling the stickers off my skin. I get up and replace the paper shirt with mine. I look to the EKG machine and wonder what it said.

After a couple minutes, a knock at the door.

"Yeah?" I say.

The door opens, and the same nurse peeks through. "Let's get you weighed."

I follow her into the hall, where a scale looms against the wall. *Damn contraption.*

"Take off your shoes," she instructs.

I bend down and pull them off my feet. I can feel the cold of the floor through my socks. Same old routine.

"Turn around."

I do.

"Now step backwards on to the scale."

'*Check out the number!*' It's Ed. I nonchalantly turn. "Step off!" the nurse says, and my chance is gone.

I follow her to the first room, where my blood was drawn before.

Motioning to the chair, she says, "Sit down."

She unhooks a blood-pressure cuff from the wall and fastens it around my arm, then presses a button. It tightens around me like a constricting snake. Right when I feel like my arm is about to fall off, it makes a hissing sound and lets go.

She pinches my small wrist, searching for a pulse. Once she's found it, she taps it into the computer.

"Stand up," she orders.

When I rise, the blood-pressure cuff slips off my bicep, and I have to catch it before it falls off my wrist. The nurse readjusts it, and it tightens again. My fingertips tingle, hurt, and go numb from it. I'm grateful when she finally takes it off and hangs it back up on the wall.

She curls her index finger around the veiny side of my wrist and clamps her thumb to the bony side. Her fingers feel rough and calloused. I search her face for any hints of what my results might be, but she's blank. Unreadable.

After several seconds, she frees my wrist and turns back to her computer. The clacking sound of her fingers flying across the keyboard fills the room. The small printer above the computer whirs to life. The nurse reaches up and plucks a paper from it, and then quickly folds it in half.

"All done," she declares. "I'm going to give this to your mother. You can follow me out."

I awkwardly trail behind her into the waiting room, where my mom looks up from her phone. She takes the paper from the nurse but doesn't open it. "Let's go," she says.

I'm hoping to catch a glimpse of the paper, but my mom keeps it firmly folded until we get to the car. She rotates her body as she opens it so I can't see.

I don't need to see what the paper says. All that I have to read is my mom's expression. Her frown could be interpreted as disapproving. But there's pure fear in her eyes. They flick from the paper up to me, then back to the paper. The car is uncomfortably quiet.

"You've lost weight," she says, frailty in her voice.

Good. Part of me relaxes. My calorie calculations were accurate enough.

"Your blood pressure has never been this low . . ." she murmurs, unable to tear her eyes away from the paper.

"What is it?" I ask.

"Seventy over sixty."

Something inside me feels triumphant. *I'm getting closer, Ed.* He's proud, I can tell. It feels good that he's proud of me. "Oh," I say.

"You know what happens when blood pressure gets too low?" Mom sighs. She folds the paper up and puts her head in her hands. "You go into cardiac arrest. You die, Charlotte."

She takes a deep, shaky breath. "I wanted to keep you home, I really did. But we've reached a point where I just want to keep you alive."

If I go to the hospital, I'll lose all control. They'll regulate what and when I eat. They might not even let me walk too far, because it would be considered exercise. Nor do I want to think about what it would be like to live an entire city away from Mom for god knows how long.

Please don't let this be it, I think desperately.

"Let's go home," I say.

"Let's go home," Mom agrees, wiping her eyes with the back of her hand. Her mascara smudges.

We emerge from the parkade, and music returns to the car. I look out the window as Mom drives, and I think about the hospital. I think about dying, too. *'Between recovery and death, death is by far the more peaceful option,'* Ed whispers. The question is, how far am I willing to go for peace?

I think about the possibility of me going into cardiac arrest, and I feel a pang of fear in the face of death.

I think back to the razor in my bathroom. Something inside of me has shifted. I'm now stuck in this strange sort of limbo between life and death, between wanting to save myself and wanting to get sicker. I'm not ready to die. I just need a little more time before I'm ready to continue living.

I watch as everything unravels.

THINGS OVERHEARD
BEHIND CLOSED DOORS

Later that night, I lay in my bed listening to the sounds of the house.

Worried, fast-paced talking from somewhere deep in its bowels. *Is that my mom?* I slide out of my bed and sneak down the hallway, down the stairs to the main floor, and then down more stairs to the basement, following the noise. I try to blend in with the shadows. The closer I get, the louder and clearer my mom's voice gets.

It leads me to her closed office door, at the far end of the basement hallway.

I slowly approach it.

"I just don't know what we're going to do," I hear my mom's tired voice say. "We've tried giving her more snacks, we've tried increasing portion sizes . . . nothing is working."

I quash my pang of guilt. Of course it's not working. I'm winning Ed's game.

"It's all about calories. You have to keep raising them," I hear another voice say. This one is deep, and belongs to a man. I recognize it. Dr. Vernon — the one who told me to "eat some nuts." I guess he's sticking around. Until I go to Edmonton, he's all the medical support we really have.

My mom must have put him on speaker phone. She does that, sometimes, when she's really focused. She'll pace around the room and take notes while the other person speaks.

"It's only getting worse. Her weight and blood pressure are both at a new low." She tells him the numbers.

Despite the horror of the situation, I feel a small grin pull at the corners of my lips. Those numbers — that's me.

There's a pause.

"How much longer until the Edmonton assessment?" Dr. Vernon asks. The hospital seems to be on everyone's mind. Even through his professionalism, I can tell he's anxious. His voice pinched and light.

And then I realize — he doesn't think I'm going to make it to the assessment.

I imagine myself having a heart attack in my sleep. The next morning — my body stiff and cold, skin pale and firm . . . A martyr for Ed. The very best at being skinny; the winner. A legacy of beautiful, brittle bones, a testament to my strength and willpower. Fluttering joy elevating me out of my frail, motionless corpse.

I scare myself when I realize a wide, proud smile has broken out on my face.

I'm not the monster. No, Ed is.

That night, back in bed, I hear more voices through the walls, this time from Parker's room, next to mine. I strain to listen.

First, Parker's voice — small and scared. "Is Charlotte going to die?"

Then, my mom's voice, low and reassuring, but I can hear the tension beneath the surface. "No, honey. We won't let that happen."

I stare into the dark. Death is the one thing that is ultimately in my control.

The sound of sniffling—quiet, delicate tears. Sadness, a splintering in my ribs. Tears burn my eyes. There's an aching in my stomach, in my head. I'm tired of causing so much pain.

So tired.

I've polluted my own childhood, and now I'm doing the same to Parker's. He and I are so alike his sorrow is in me, like a reflection.

"Is she going to be hospitalized?" he asks.

My mom pauses. "Yes," she finally says. "That's how she's going to get better."

Just like that, all the pride I had after hearing the call with our doctor is swallowed. I'm not holy. I'm not transcending, I'm dying. These organs inside me are failing. I'm going to wake up dead and cold, and there will be no victory. There will be a dead fifteen-year-old girl and her crying little brother.

All of Ed's ego and honour is sucked out of me, and I feel very small and incredibly scared.

For just a moment, Ed's tainted view of the joys of starvation dissipates. Game to nightmare. I'm left wondering which one it really is.

I *spend the night* with my eyes glued to my phone. Too immersed in what I'm watching to sleep—a deep pit of dread has settled into my stomach. I'm watching YouTube videos about in-patient treatment.

It sounds horrible, barely possible. *Surely this can't happen to me.* But here it is. My potential future, documented and summarized in a ten-minute video.

A girl on the screen talks about how mealtimes are

in groups, and sometimes people get really upset while eating. I can barely handle keeping myself together while eating — I'm not sure I'd be able to watch other people suffer like that. She also explains a normal day at the hospital — therapy, medication, and a lot of eating. There'd be lots of high-calorie liquid-meal-replacements, too (which are infamously disgusting. Wasted calories).

Eventually, I can't take it anymore. I turn off my phone and rest it on my chest as I rub at my glassy eyes. I can't go to that living hell. I'd sooner die than let them take me.

EMERGENCY

Years ago, my grandpa bought a monitoring cuff to track his rising blood pressure. My grandpa is seventy. He's lived a long life, and has come to understand the concept of mortality.

After changing some lifestyle habits, though, he's gotten his blood pressure back down to a healthy level, and no longer has much use for the cuff. My mom has asked to borrow it, and now, a couple evenings later, it's around my frail arm, where there was once muscle. Even at its tightest, it still slides down, and I have to hold it in place with my other arm.

Why am I wearing this blood-pressure cuff so young? I've only lived for fifteen years, and I already understand what a fragile, temporary thing life is. I'm too young for all this. I should be out, living my teenage years with abandon, taking risks as if I'll live forever. This illness has robbed me of the blissful oblivion of youth.

I'm lying on my bed. The cuff constricts. I've never felt this awful before. I'm weak, so fucking weak. My mind is fuzzy, and I can't seem to think clearly. I close my eyes, exhale.

Beep beep beep beep, and the cuff loosens with a hissing sound. Normally, I'd try to get a peek at my blood pressure, eagerly curious about how good I was at having an eating disorder. Not today. I stay hiding in the darkness beneath my eyelids, darkness I keep returning too. I'm so exhausted. I want to fall asleep — if sleep can come.

How have things taken such a sudden turn for the worse?

I hear my mom inhale sharply. "Let's go to emergency."

Even the act of sitting up is difficult. When I stand, the edges of my vision tinge purple. I try to say, *What's that supposed to mean?*

One foot in front of the other, my mom hauls me to the garage. Before we leave, she scribbles a quick note and leaves it on the counter for Parker and Dad. We get in the car and pull out of the driveway. I lean against the window as we drive, feeling the cold glass press against my forehead.

Surely this body isn't mine.

The world passing outside my window blurs into a rush of buildings and lampposts. People walking their dogs, pushing strollers, riding bikes. Normal life, passing by. Everything I've isolated myself from. Everything I can't be a part of. Soon, I can see the hospital looming ahead.

What happens next is a blur.

A young woman sits at a desk beside me, typing into a computer turned away from me. Her hard eyes peer out from above her mask, and she occasionally glances over. The lights inside the room are blindingly bright. I barely speak; my mom explains the whole situation to her.

"But has she been *diagnosed*?" the woman asks.

I'm moved to a waiting room. Listlessly, I stare at my shoes. I hate this place.

I blink, and when I next open my eyes, I'm lying in a hospital bed. I recoil against the burning, utilitarian light above.

A female voice says, "Good thing she came in today," and disappears.

Is this it?

A man in a medical uniform leans over me, a dark figure obstructing the light. He's pulling up my shirt and pressing his fingers into my stomach. "I can feel your spine through your stomach!" he says.

Unsure what else to do, I give a half-hearted smile.

He's reaching across me and pressing cold EKG stickers all along my ribs, across my bare chest, one on each arm, one on my leg.

I'm a pile of bones lying in a nest of medical cords.

My body doesn't belong to me. It's stuck, torn between this dangerous illness and the medical professionals, each side fighting for control. I'm completely out of the equation — I have no say.

Another blood pressure cuff is fastened to my arm. This one squeezes until I feel my hand go numb.

The man's saying something — I try to focus — ". . . be with you shortly." All I can do is nod.

He's gone. How cold the room is; I begin to shiver. I reach down to pull up the thin, scratchy blanket folded at the foot of the bed. I move gingerly, so as not to disconnect any of the EKG patches. The blanket provides no warmth.

Somehow, though, beneath this dazed, disconnected suffering, there is peace — I'm starting to feel it. I'm so close — so close to the eye of the storm.

A TV is attached to the wall across from me, playing *The Backyardigans*. I try to focus on it, to listen to the voices of the characters I used to watch when I was a little girl, but the beeping of all the machines is drowning out any chance of me hearing the audio; they're suffocating me with their constant, rhythmic sounds, reminding me of where I am, reminding me of what my life has come to.

My head feels like static on a TV.

I wonder if I'm going to die.

I'm dipping in and out of reality — one second I'm here, another second I'm sinking back into my own consciousness. My vision of the room shrinks. My eyes lower into slits. I know I should be scared, but I don't have the energy to feel at all. My god, I'm so tired.

I waver in and out. Has my body ever really belonged to me? Maybe I'm nothing but Ed's property. Maybe that's what I've been all along.

Time passes, I'm not sure how much. I can hear my mom and a doctor talking.

"If she's not actively in cardiac arrest, there's nothing we can do here in the ER. You're free to go," a doctor says.

"Look at her blood pressure, though!" my mom exclaims.

"I'm sorry, ma'am. Would you like her to be transferred to the eating disorder ward?" he asks.

Here? In Calgary? I think back to what Michelle told me about that place. *Oh god, please no.*

"No, thank you," my mom says. "We've got a referral to the Edmonton ward."

And just like that, my mom and I are on our way out, heading to the car.

Like nothing ever happened — is happening.

Like my blood pressure isn't at a deadly low.

Like I'm not on death's doorstep.

I leave that horrible hospital room, but I feel like I've forgotten part of me inside, like how you might forget your coat or your phone. I worry part of me will always be trapped in that hospital room.

THE BASEMENT

It's early evening by the time we return home. I fall asleep, relieved to find myself in the Deep. Real life is so complicated. It's complicated in the Deep, too, but at least it's a different kind of complicated.

My feet touch the cold wood of the floor as I slide out of bed. I wonder what the Mysterious Girl will have to say tonight, after seeing those vitals. My body moves with ease here, unrestricted by the shackles of reality.

I creep through the sleeping house. The distant sound of a clock hasn't gone away.

Tick. Tick. Tick.

Where is it coming from?

I wander down through the town. It's even quieter than usual. No one seems to be out tonight. It's just me and the dark night. My stomach shoots pain. "Hello?" I call out. My voice echoes off the houses.

The voice of a boy answers me, so quiet it's barely a whisper. "Hello."

Or maybe that was just the strange workings of the echoes.

I keep walking. Each footstep sounds thunderous in comparison to the quiet of the town. I'm waiting for the Mysterious Girl to pop out onto the street, but she's nowhere.

Above me, a cloud passes over the moon, and everything turns black. My heart is beginning to thud in my chest. A thin glimmer of moonlight shines through the cloud, just enough to reveal a figure standing perfectly still in the middle of the road.

The moon once again is covered, and we're enveloped in darkness.

"It's dangerous out here, you know." It's a male voice — his speaking precise and raspy.

I feel the bent-up tightness inside of me loosen a little. "Ed, is that you?" I ask.

"Yes, Charlotte. It's me."

As long as Ed's here, he'll protect me. He'll numb me from any unpleasant feeling life can throw at me, he'll lend me his strength.

Still, I feel my fight-or-flight senses kicking in. My body is telling me to run. But I don't; I don't know what safety means anymore.

Can he feel my presence the way I can feel his?

It's so dark my eyes might as well be closed. Anything could attack me here; I'd never see it coming. I rotate in circles, trying to spot danger, but it's no use. My senses are failing me. I'm completely vulnerable.

"I'm scared," I whisper.

"Yes, be scared. You have a lot to fear." I can hear footsteps. Ed, walking towards me.

The sound of his footsteps is disorienting. Is he circling around me? The air is turning cold and stale. Every bone in my body feels paralyzed.

"The world is a horrible place, Charlotte, filled with horrible people who do horrible things. It's no place for vulnerability. No place for innocence." Ed pauses thoughtfully. "It's no place for you."

The cloud moves past the moon, revealing Ed, standing right in front of me. His skin pale in the moonlight. Ghostly.

I glance around the street. The townspeople are inside, standing by their windows.

They stare out at me with blank expressions.

Ed gently places his hands over mine. They're icy and soft. "I can protect you," he promises. "Keep you safe from all of it." He looks me in the eyes, and asks me, "Will you accept my protection?"

The muscles in my neck seize up as I nod.

"I know a safe place," he comforts me. "Follow me." Still lightly holding on to my hand, he leads me down the street.

The shadows change shape as I approach them. They morph into monsters with human figures.

They infest corners, doorways, alleys . . .

Everything.

All of the Deep has turned into one seething, black malevolent shadow.

"Feel the darkness breathing?"

I tightly squeeze Ed's hand.

"Don't worry." His voice is soothing. "I'm going to be here for you. Always."

A sudden turn. He guides me down a dark alleyway.

Shadows swarm, but Ed's pale skin glows through the darkness like a flashlight. The shadows hiss and recoil as he approaches. He wards them off.

The pavement is scattered with an array of detritus. I step over broken glass and cigarette butts. Strange faces have been graffitied onto the walls on either side. They watch me as I walk by them.

I look at Ed, navigating the darkness in front of us. *Save me from this madness.* The deeper we go into the alleyway, the darker it gets. Not even moonlight can reach this crevice of the Deep.

The only way I'm able to see is by the light emanating from Ed's skin.

The ground beneath my feet is now littered with empty beer bottles and needles. My foot sinks into something soft. I bend down and pick up the teddy bear from my childhood. It's been ripped and stained beyond repair. Stuffing falls from the gashes and through my fingers, bleeding out of the bear.

"No!" I cry, trying to catch the stuffing before it falls, but it's no use. Soon, my bear is completely empty. I hold its limp fabric in my hands and stare at it through tears.

When I look up, Ed is eyeing me empathetically. He lifts the bear from my hands. I let him. He kisses the bear's forehead, then gently lays its deflated body back on the filthy ground. "It's gone," he tells me.

We keep moving forwards. Goosebumps pimple my skin, and I'm shivering hard. I grip Ed's hand, desperate for his reassurance.

We come to a rusted door. Ed reaches out, taps it open. "In here," he says. "It's our little safe haven."

Trembling, I step through the doorway. In front of me, stairs lead down into a dark abyss. Not even a trace of light. Ed kicks the door closed behind us, and I hear the clicking of a lock. I turn around and look at him. "To keep the monsters out," he says. "Now, go on."

I edge down the stairs. Sweat and tears are dripping from my face.

Suddenly, two cold hands thrust into my shoulders. I lose my balance and tumble forwards. The edges of the stairs hit my exposed bones as I fall. My limbs thrash, slam into each other.

My screams echo throughout whatever this strange place is. The echoes won't let my screams die.

My head smashes against a cold concrete floor, and

everything

goes

black.

When I wake up, sharp pain is splintering through my head. I have double vision. Everything sounds like it's underwater.

As my sight returns, I see the boy, no more than bones wrapped in a parcel of skin, standing in front of me. His greasy black hair dangles in front of his face as he leans in towards me, inspecting me with his dead eyes.

"Hello, Charlotte," he says, his voice low. My hearing has returned enough for me to make out the words. "Welcome back."

I look around. I've been tied to a wooden chair with dirty rags. I strain against them, but it's no use. I'm too weak. Ed chuckles at my pitiful attempt.

I'm in an unfinished basement. The dingy, stained walls drip. A thin strip of filthy window near the ceiling looks out onto the dark street. The rotting stench of death.

"What do you want from me?" I ask through gritted teeth.

"I just want to be your friend." Ed smiles. "And keep you safe."

"Keep me safe?" My voice is strangled.

In a flash of movement, his bony hands curl around my throat. I gasp for air.

He leans in close to my ear. "It's so much better in here. I'm protecting you from things far worse." He pulls his head back and looks me in the eyes. "Horrible things await you in the real world, Charlotte. You have to trust me." He releases my neck.

"I *did* trust you!" I scream. An emptiness in my stomach. A lump in my throat. I've ruined so much of myself for Ed.

I try to rock my chair over, break free of the rags, anything that I think will free me. Nothing works. Ed looks amused.

"I'll wake up tomorrow morning!" I shriek at him. "And when I wake up in the Deep next week, I *will* avoid you!"

Ed plays with the ratty window blind, then shakes his head. "You don't seem to understand." So calm. Eyes trailing over my body. "If you're still in this room, in my possession by the time the sun rises in the real world, Charlotte." He pauses. "You won't wake up."

I'm not ready to go. But I've already been in the Deep for too long.

"*Help! Somebody help me!*" I holler. But my voice is whispery and hoarse.

Ed leans back against the wall across from me, sinks down. He sits there watching me.

I realize I'm never going to have the chance to say goodbye to Mom.

GLASS

The longer I'm in the room, the weaker I get. It starts to spin and contort like a funhouse mirror, black dots appearing like flies swarming a dead animal. I'm going to vomit.

There can't be much time left. Hope seeps out between my bones. In the real world, is the sun breaking over the horizon? Let it. Just make this suffering end.

So this is what it feels like to starve yourself to death. Thoughts foggy, contaminated. My body is drained of energy. I'm slumped over, crushed by the weight of gravity, bones digging into bones. Is the body already dead? Me, nothing but a sick mind leaking from an empty shell.

Movement out one of the ceiling-level windows. A *rat*.

Except there's two. One moves, then the other. Back and forth, back and forth, moving along the window's length. They shine slightly through the darkness. Are they . . . shoes?

The strange shapes stop — seen them — where?

Can't form coherent thought. I try to dive into my memory, slipping through my fingers as I grab.

Powerful running . . .

One odd, detached snippet of a memory. But it's something. What else, what else?

Dancing . . .

Elegant dancing . . .

No . . . could it really be?

I look up at the shoes just in time to see them kicking through the glass window. Glass sprays everywhere, and Ed jolts upright, instinctively covering his face and stumbling backwards against the wall.

I see a girl slip down through the window. The glass tears through her skin as she falls into the basement. When she stands back up, her body drips thin trails of blood.

I meet those blue-green eyes. For a second it's almost like I'm looking into a mirror.

The Mysterious Girl.

My mind is barely processing fast enough — what's happening? The Mysterious Girl charges Ed, who looks completely startled and unprepared. They're yelling things at each other, but I can't make out the words.

Despite his attempts to wiggle free, she forcefully grabs his head with both her hands and slams it against the wall. He falls to the ground in a crumpled heap.

She's running towards me. Hands fumbling for my wrists. She's searching for a pulse.

I manage to lift my head just enough to show her I'm alive. She grabs a shard of glass from the broken window, cuts through the rags that tie me to the chair.

I barely make out her words through the chaos. "— have to go, he'll wake up soon." She gathers my frail body up into her arms and lifts me out the window, settling me on to the cold, damp alleyway outside and scrambles out after me.

Behind her, I hear Ed starting to stir.

The Mysterious Girl swoops me up in her arms again and begins to run. I curl up against her bloodied chest. The rhythmic thump of her fast steps jolt through my body.

Thump thump thump thump thump.

trust

/trəst/

noun

1. firm belief in the reliability, truth, ability, or strength of someone or something.

CONFESSION

The next morning, I wake up.

That's all that matters.

My entire body aches and throbs after last night, so the first thing I do is get some Advil from my bathroom cabinet.

I go downstairs to find Mom rushing around the kitchen, frazzled. Golden sunlight streams in through the window. Gratitude is warm in my chest.

"Good morning!" Mom exclaims with a smile. She pushes a heaping bowl of sugared nuts, oats, and cranberries towards me. "I made a fresh batch of granola for you, for breakfast." She looks nervous as she awaits my response.

I remember the horrors of last night. I remember what got me there.

"Thanks, Mom," I say with a smile. I get some milk from the fridge and pour it over the granola and sit down to eat it. My arm tenses up at first, unwilling to deliver the spoon to my mouth. When I taste the nutty flavours on my tongue, tears begin to blur the edges of my vision; I hastily wipe them. Deep breath. It's difficult, but I know now the consequences of skipping. I try to put my body on autopilot and not think about what I'm doing. It's just a series of motions. Spoon in my bowl, spoon in my mouth, repeat.

It's almost funny how surprised Mom looks.

After school, I go to therapy.

"Hey, how have you been?" Michelle asks as we head to her office.

We both sit down, and I cross my legs beneath me.

"I feel guilty," I admit, and it's true. I haven't been honest with the most important people to me.

"And why's that?" She leans forwards slightly.

"I've been skipping meals," I say.

"Your parents are letting you?"

"No, I've been lying about eating them." I explain the whole routine I've built myself, involving sneaking snacks back into the pantry and dumping chocolate milk down the sink to claim the empty carton as 'proof' of my consumption.

"Well, that explains your lack of weight gain." Michelle adds sincerely, "I think we should tell your parents."

"I don't think so." *My god, they'll be so mad.*

"Do you live close?" she asks.

"Yes."

"Would your mom be able to drive here right now?"

"Bad idea."

"It will all be under control. I'll guide everything, and make sure she doesn't get mad," Michelle reassures. "Otherwise, the doctors are going to think that you need even more calories, and you'll start skipping even more, and it will all be a vicious cycle."

I stare at her uncertainly. That's a good point, but that doesn't necessarily make it a good idea.

"Okay?" she says.

I'm not expecting this to go well, but I trust her. "Okay."

Fifteen minutes later, Mom shows up at the door. Michelle takes her to her office. I hide in the waiting room. I scroll through my phone without really looking at anything, pick at my cuticles, read the posters on the walls, anything to get my mind off the conversation that's happening in the office.

Time passes brutally slowly.

Finally, Michelle sticks her head into the waiting room. "Come on in," she says. She looks relatively calm and chipper, but you never know. That could just be to disguise her fear of my mom's rage. I imagine my mom yelling at me the moment I enter the room ("I *trusted you,* Charlotte! I *trusted you!*"), but when I shuffle inside, she's sitting peacefully on the couch.

Surprised, I sit down beside her, waiting for the lecture. It never comes.

Instead, Mom says, "I'm glad you 'fessed up," and squeezes my hand.

I blink at her. "'You're not mad?"

"Of course I'm not. It was really brave of you to tell Michelle." She gives me a warm smile. "This skipping can't continue, though. It's dangerous, with where you are right now."

"I know. I'm not gonna do it anymore," I say, relieved at how calm this all is turning out. I glance over at Michelle.

She has worked her magic.

STARS

That night, I sit by my open window, looking up at the dark sky. The night sky in this world is nowhere near as spectacular as the night sky in the Deep, but it still feels peaceful.

I think about my situation — this whole mess — and try to make sense of it.

I look over to my bathroom. The razor shines faintly through the darkness, and I remember what life felt like that night.

I can't kill Ed with a blade. He's buried himself too deep within me, in the darkest crevices of my mind; in my struggling pulse; in the pale, drained colour of my face. He hides among the obsessive thoughts that repeat in my head over and over; he meddles and tinkers with the hardwiring of my brain, creating a horrible, selfish, primitive being whose goal is to be the world's thinnest girl, whose goal is to die . . .

How do I extricate myself from him?

In all honesty, I don't know if there is a way. But if there is, I must try to find it. A razor will not help me.

Six nights later, I wake up in the Deep. The Mysterious Girl is sitting in the corner of the room, reading a book. She looks up and smiles at me when she sees I'm awake. I'm glad she's here. If she wasn't, I would've locked myself in the house, protecting myself from the strange and scary world that I've learned the Deep can be.

"How are you feeling?" she asks, setting her book down.

"Good . . . A little sore, though," I admit.

"That's all?"

"Well, a little scared, too."

She nods.

"Have you just been sitting there and waiting for me?" I ask.

"I promised to protect you, did I not?"

"Thank you," I say.

She gets to her feet and walks over to the window. Looks out at the meadow, her back to me.

"Never follow Ed again," she warns. "If you do, I might not be able to save you in time."

"I'll try, I really will," I promise. "It's just so tempting . . ."

"You like the way it feels to be around him, don't you?" she says.

I nod, and get out of bed to join her at the window. "He's like an addiction," I say. "Like I'm addicted to being thin."

"That's true," the Mysterious Girl agrees. "You get addicted to certain feelings. You get addicted to certain people." Here, her eyes settle briefly on the bench in the meadow. "You get addicted to a life you can't have. And one of these days, if you don't get control over it, it's going to kill you."

I watch the leaves of the oak tree swish from a distance. "You can't be Ed. You saved me from him," I realize.

"That's true."

"You want the best for me, don't you?" I ask.

"Yes, but you have to want the best for yourself, first."

"Who are you?" I beg again.

She reaches out and opens my window, letting in the fresh air and the sound of crickets. "I have an idea," she says with a grin, looking over at me. "Follow me."

She climbs up onto the windowsill, balancing on the small section of roofing that comes down over the back door.

"Careful!" I exclaim.

From there, she reaches up and grabs hold of the roof above the window. Pulling herself with her arms, she wiggles up, until she disappears onto the roof above. Stunned, I look out my window and up to the roof.

Her head pokes out over the edge above. Eyes alive and playful. "Come on! It'll be fun!"

I nervously step out my window and onto the shingles above the back door. It feels slippery beneath my feet. *Don't look down.* With shaking hands, I grab hold of the roof above my window, not sure I'll have the strength to pull myself up.

"Here, grab on." The Mysterious Girl extends a hand off the edge. I feel the looming drop beneath my feet.

This is crazy.

But I hold onto her hand, squeeze it so tightly I wouldn't be surprised if she loses all circulation. She hauls me up onto the roof. I sit down on the cold shingles and scoot away from the edge.

When I glance over at the Mysterious Girl, her neck is craned upwards, staring at the sky. I look up too, and everything seems to go quiet. The sky is alive with stars. They pierce through the darkness, swirled with dust of periwinkle and faint white. It's an explosion of light and colour.

"Whoa."

Still looking up, the Mysterious Girl lies down. I do, too.

"What are we going to do?" I sigh.

"Suffer," she answers calmly. "But I like to think we'll suffer for a purpose."

A peaceful silence falls.

"It's almost like I could reach out and touch the stars," I murmur. They're so beautiful it's hard to imagine we exist in the same universe.

"Try it," the Mysterious Girl says.

"What?"

She repeats, "You're in your mind. Anything is possible. Try it. Touch the stars."

I focus on a specific star — a bright speck of silvery light above. I feel slightly embarrassed — am I really going to try to touch something thousands of light-years away? Still, I reach up. I put my index finger and thumb around the air in front of the star. Carefully, I pinch down. Warmth blossoms between the pads of my fingers. I bring them down to my eyes and examine the little ball of light I'm holding.

Astonished, I look over at the Mysterious Girl. "Are you seeing this?" I ask.

"You're doing it," she says with a grin. "You're controlling the Deep."

I let go of the star and watch as it floats back up to its place in the sky.

Something in the Mysterious Girl's eyes lights up. "I have an idea," she declares.

"Oh no."

"No, it's a great one. Do you want to do something kind of insane?" she asks.

"What do you mean?" I ask nervously. I thought we just did.

She stands and treks up the roof until she's at its highest point. "Ready?" she says, energy and eagerness alight in her eyes.

"What are you doing?" I say uneasily. I'm not so certain this idea is going to end well.

Suddenly, she sprints down the roof, legs pumping. Charging straight towards its edge.

"No! Stop!" I holler, racing to tackle her. But I trip, and skin my knees as I catch my fall. Turn just in time to see her fly off the roof.

Silence.

I scramble to my feet, rushing to peer over the edge, when suddenly, she bursts upwards into the sky. I'm so startled I nearly fall backwards.

She sails by, clothes flapping in the breeze. She flies in loops, curving through the night like a bird.

"You're flying!" I exclaim.

"Well, obviously!" she calls with a smile and a wink. She hovers thirty feet in the air, gently kicking her legs as if treading water. "Come on! Your turn!"

Anxiously, I look over the edge of the roof to the massive drop below, the void of empty space looming beneath me.

"You have more control than you credit yourself with," she encourages. "Now help me prove my point!"

I climb back up to the highest part of the roof and stare down at my runway of shingles.

Then, all of a sudden, I'm sprinting at full speed — like there is no drop, only an endless amount of roof.

I gain momentum and try not to think about the fall.

I *picked a star from the sky. Now I can fly.*

I squeeze my eyes shut.

There's nothing I can do but trust myself.

I leap

And plummet

    down

        down

            down.

Something catches me. Before I can fully register what's happening, I'm swooping upwards, soaring into the stars. I open my eyes and see all the colours of the illuminated night sky rushing towards me.

"You're doing it!" I hear the Mysterious Girl exclaim.

I weave between the stars, bursting through pale clouds of space dust suspended in the sky. Everything around me glowing. The fresh night air fills my lungs, charged with exhilaration. The wind blows my hair back from my face.

"This is amazing!" I hoot.

The Mysterious Girl is smiling broadly as she watches me. The stars are sparkling in her eyes.

I soar above the town, free of the restraints of gravity. A joyful, childlike energy swelling in my chest. Cool night air filters through my extended fingers. My heart is racing with excitement.

This is it — this is what it's all for.

I surge upwards, passing by floating stars. I'm moving so fast they're nothing but streaks of light in my peripheral vision. I'm going higher, and higher, and higher, and —

I **open** **my** **eyes** to my bedroom ceiling. This morning, I wake up smiling.

nos·tal·gia

/näˈstaljə, nəˈstaljə/

noun

1. a sentimental longing or wistful affection for the past, typically for a period or place with happy personal associations.

THE BUS STOP

A *week later*, I look out my bedroom window, searching for those stars that made me feel immortal in the Deep. It's too cloudy to see much of anything.

I wish there was a way I could hit pause tonight.

A way to stop tomorrow from coming.

Tomorrow morning, I'll have to wake up, have breakfast, and get in the car to go to Edmonton for the assessment.

I can't help but hate myself for the connection I've formed with Ed. I led myself to this fate, fully aware of what I was doing. Now, not only am I going to be fattened and lose the only sense of security I have, but I'm also going to do so surrounded by people as sick and sicker than me. They might shove a feeding tube up my nose and down my throat, something I've heard is horribly painful.

This is it.

My phone buzzes from my bed, and I walk over and pick it up. It's Jade.

Are you still waiting until tomorrow to
find out if you're going to Edmonton?

It's been weeks since we last texted. I answer:

Yes. It's quite the suspenseful wait.

I've been thinking about you, and I really
hope everything works out okay. What
time will you find out?

Thanks :)
The appointment is at 1pm.

You don't have to answer, but what would you be going for?

It might make you sad.

I still want to know.

For some reason, I can't bring myself to type it out. I don't really know why, after all the destruction Ed has caused me, I can't just type out his name. I want to tell her, though. Something about it is so parasitic and vile. Typing it out and sending it as a text would make it even more immortal than it already is.

I have an idea.

Its presence in my mind is so unexpected I have to think about it for a couple moments to be sure I really want to send it to Jade.

I decide I do.

Do you want to meet in person?

Now?

Yeah.

I stare at my phone, nervously awaiting a response.

Yes.

I look at the clock beside my bed. Almost exactly midnight. Through text, Jade and I agree to meet halfway between our houses.

I pull over a hoodie and zip up a jacket in an attempt to protect myself from the cold.

I creep downstairs, and freeze. My dad is asleep on the couch, snoring. I carefully slink around him. What would I even say if he woke up? *'Hey, Dad, I'm just going for a walk in the cold in the dead of night.'* I slowly unlock the back door, a subtle grinding sound of metal on metal; I wince, open the back door, and close it softly behind me.

I'm met with the chilly night air. Something about its sharp coldness awakens something inside of me. It reminds me that I'm here — alive.

Just like that, I'm on my way.

Moonlight basking the house reminds me of the Deep. My heart pounds in my chest as I walk away from it and into the darkness. The route goes through a park space, so there aren't any streetlights for the majority of it. I scan the shadows ahead and curl my hands into fists, just in case. Every once in a while, I glance over my shoulder.

It's just me, alone with the darkness.

Until I see Jade approaching the other side of the park, and I'm no longer alone.

She's also bundled in many layers of clothing. She's changed her haircut from when we were together all that time ago, but her eyes remain the same — forest green.

I smile at her. "Hey," I say as we meet in the middle of the park space.

"Hey," she says, smiling back. Her cheeks are slightly rosy from the cold. She smells like that combination of jasmine and vanilla, just like she did before.

The scent that once gave me nervous elation.

The scent that later felt like a knife twisting into my chest.

Tonight, I don't know what it makes me feel. Maybe simply grateful.

"Where should we go?" she asks.

I look over her shoulder towards a bus stop by the road. "A heated bus shelter?"

"Good idea."

She glances over at my jacket. I'm pretty sure she's wearing three.

"There's no way you're gonna be warm enough," she says. "You've always been a naturally chilly person."

"That's where the heated bus shelter comes in," I say.

The bus shelter is like a little glass rectangle by the side of the road with doors on each side and a contemporary wood and metal roof. There's a little bench to sit on that faces the road, and behind that bench, two prints of bizarre modern art that have been secured within the glass wall.

Jade opens one of the doors and holds it ajar for me.

"Thanks." I step inside. I press the little button to turn on the heaters, which rest in the top corners of the shelter. They burn red as they spring to life. Warmth radiates down on to my face. I crane my neck towards them, trying to soak up as much of the heat as possible.

"Whoever thought of these heated bus shelters deserves a raise," I say.

"Ahh, the bench is cold," Jade says as she lowers herself on to the metal slab.

I sit down beside her. She's right — the cold pierces through my sweatpants.

She leans back against the glass. I do the same.

Say it, I tell myself. *Say the word. Tell her.* But for some reason, my voice feels stuck in my throat.

We watch as cars on the road zoom past us — their headlights getting bigger and brighter as they approach, their taillights growing fainter, smaller as they disappear back into the night.

"What is it?" she asks softly.

I'm quiet for a second. Then, I choke out the horrible word: "*Anorexia.*"

She nods thoughtfully.

My left leg begins to shake uncontrollably. My eyes burn with the familiar promise of tears. I think of the threatening hospital I'll be driving to tomorrow. I think about how I willingly held Ed's hand and followed him. "I can't believe I've done this to myself."

"Whoa," Jade says, sits up, and looks me in the eyes. "This is *not* your fault."

"It kinda is." If someone had told me a couple months ago that it wasn't, I would've agreed. But tonight, as I await the repercussions of my actions that will take place tomorrow, I feel guilty of committing a horrible crime.

"You never chose this," Jade says firmly.

And then I realize, that's true.

My leg is shaking even harder now, but I barely pay it attention. I wipe at my eyes with the back of my hand and sniffle my running noise. "I'm gonna have a little mental breakdown now," I say with a sad smile.

"It's okay. I had a mental breakdown earlier today and tried to dye my hair blue," Jade says, laughing gently.

I look closer at her hair. Under the bright lighting of the bus shelter against the dark of the night, her dark brown hair does have a slightly colder shade to it. "Oh yeah! I can kind of see it!" I exclaim.

"It didn't really show up, for which I'm now extremely grateful. Let's just say it's a good thing I have dark hair," she says with a smile.

"No, I like it. It looks nice," I assure her.

She gives a slight laugh. "Thanks." Then her face turns serious again, and she asks, "When did it start?"

When *did* it start? I've been asking myself that question a lot recently, but I just don't know. There was no definitive moment—it was a long slope that I just sort of gradually slid down until I found myself at the bottom of a crevice. "Maybe nine months ago," I say.

She's silent for a moment. Then, quietly, she asks, "It wasn't me, was it?"

"No." In all honesty, I don't know. I don't know what started this chain of events that led me here. It was a horrible feeling, having two of the most important people in my life turn against me so unexpectedly. What difference will any of it make now? What's done is done. I say it just as much for my sake as hers. She had just been trying her best, and I forgive her completely.

"I'm scared for the hospital," I whisper.

She puts her index finger out in the air. Confused, I stare at it for a second. Then I touch the tip of my index finger against hers. "I'm transferring positive energy to you," Jade says. We stay like that for a moment, looking at our fingers and smiling.

If I had a grain of sand for every time you made me cry, I'd have a desert. But if I had a star for every time you made me smile, I'd have the entire universe.

Eventually, the cold begins to nip at my finger, so we return our hands back into our pockets.

Jade tells me stories about her stay in the hospital. It sounds like something a producer would make a gritty reality TV show about.

Seeing as I'm going to Edmonton, and would be in the eating disorder ward, my experience would probably be much different, but there's still something amusing and vaguely comforting about the way she describes it all. We watch cars whoosh past us as we talk. It's like the bus shelter is a bubble, where in that moment, nothing outside of it exists.

By one o'clock, my fingers and toes are beginning to sting from the cold. "I'm getting a little chilly. I might call it a night soon," I say. I'm getting tired.

"Yeah, me too," Jade agrees.

I stand up and open the bus shelter door for her, and we step outside. The night is even colder without the protection of the heaters.

"Goodnight," I say with a smile.

"Bye," she says.

I turn around, and am about to start walking home, when I suddenly hear her exclaim, "Wait!"

I turn back around just in time to see her running towards me. She wraps her arms around me, and I hug her back. I feel something warm blossom in my chest. We hold each other.

Something beautiful that shattered into painful, unfixable shards.

But sometimes shards will catch the light.

HEARTBEAT

I wake up in the Deep to a steady, pounding vibration in the ground. At first, I think it's an earthquake, but it's too consistent, too repetitious. I run through the house and out the back door, standing in the meadow in my bare feet. The grass beneath my toes is soft.

I still hear the vibrations, though. Now I feel them in my feet, too. It's not the house — it's some greater force in the Deep.

I don't know how I know the Mysterious Girl is sitting on the other side of the oak tree trunk, but I do. I can sense her presence, the same way I can sometimes sense Ed's.

I wander through the dark meadow towards her, pass by where the bench used to be, but now, in its place, is a lone heated bus shelter.

Sure enough, there she is, leaning back against the bark. The Mysterious Girl gives me a small grin, but there's nervousness brewing in her eyes. "Hello."

"Hey. What's that pounding in the ground?" I ask.

The Mysterious Girl puts her hand down against the grass and closes her eyes, letting the reverberations charge through the tips of her fingers and up into her body. "It's a heartbeat," she answers.

"A heartbeat?"

"Your heartbeat, to be specific."

"Why?" I press.

"You're on the brink of hospitalization, but you're still

alive. I can only guess that some force of the Deep wants you to remember that."

"Hmm." I sit down beside her. "Tomorrow's the big day." I sigh.

"You're nervous, aren't you?" Her voice is low and empathetic.

"Very."

"For the first time, everyone in the Deep can agree with you. I'm just as nervous."

"Even Ed?" I ask.

"Especially Ed," she confirms.

There's no way to tell what will happen tomorrow. I've been working hard to make progress ever since I was held in that basement, but has it been *enough*? Nothing ever seems to be enough. It's a constant uphill battle.

"Do you think they'll take me?" I ask. The field of grass sways with a detached, faded haze, like shallow brush-strokes in a dark painting.

"I don't know. They might," she answers. "Either way, there's nothing we can do about it. We have no control."

"That's why I hate it so much," I sigh, rubbing my eyes tiredly. "What if I run away?"

"If you run, the police will come looking for you. That's what they do when you're medically unstable and unaccounted for," the Mysterious Girl points out. "I'll warn you, you're going to have to be careful. Ed is scared, and when he's scared, he does drastic and irrational things."

"What do you mean?" I ask.

"The three of us — we have a sort of shared knowledge. If they hospitalize you, Ed is going to try to convince you to hurt yourself. Badly."

I shiver. "Will I have a choice, this time?"

Above us, a flutter of glossy back feathers. A raven swoops down from the sky and perches on one of the oak tree's branches. I look up — it cocks its head slightly, as if it too is waiting for an answer.

She frowns grimly. "I honestly don't know."

The raven caws — a flat, somber sound — and flies away.

I know where she's coming from — I've been feeling the impacts of Ed's thoughts. I'm more afraid of the hospital than death. Or is it that I'm more afraid of suffering than death? Both, I suppose.

How did I get into this mess?

I imagine my heart falling from a gaping hole in my chest.

I press my hand against the grassy ground, and feel the heartbeat of the Deep, of me.

Tha-thump. Tha-thump. Tha-thump.

I focus on the way it buzzes through my fingers. I let it fill the silence, let it fill my mind.

The Mysterious Girl pulls out her scratched gold watch from her pocket and flicks it open. "Time's almost up," she says.

"I'm not ready. I'm not ready for tomorrow. I'm not ready to go."

"You're going to make it through, okay?"

"Okay." She has no way of knowing.

"I want you to do something for me," she says.

"What is it?"

"When you're in Edmonton, I want you to clasp your

hands together. Like this." She grasps one of her hands with the other.

I look at her curiously.

She gives me a sad smile. "That'll be me. That'll be me, holding your hand."

The Mysterious Girl glances down to her watch. "Good luck, Charlotte."

I wake up to the sound of my alarm clock playing a radio song. My heart beats heavy in my chest.

Tha-thump. Tha-thump. Tha-thump.

Today's the day.

sol·i·tude

/ˈsälə̵t(y)o͞od/

noun

1. the state or situation of being alone.

THE CLINIC

It's a three-hour drive to Edmonton from Calgary. Darkness shrouds us when we leave. "Bro-hug?" Parker says as I get my boots on at the back door. There are bags under his eyes, pupils clouded by early-morning exhaustion. I try for a brave smile and grab his hand, pull him in.

I brought a book to read in the car, but I can't focus enough to read it. I'm too nervous. Instead, I rest my head against the window in the back seat, headphones on, and watch the rest of the world slowly wake up.

Anticipation ripples through me, jittery and nauseous. I pick absentmindedly at my cuticles until they bleed.

I'd secretly been hoping for awful traffic — we could've been late and missed the appointment — but our car is zooming along. There's nothing between Edmonton and me but a shrinking number of kilometres.

"Do you remember your questions, Charlotte?" my mom asks from the driver's seat. My parents have made a list of all the questions they want to ask, and I've made one, too.

"Yeah," I mumble. I already know I'm not going to like the answers.

I'm scared.

Ed is scared.

The Mysterious Girl is scared.

Nothing good can come from this.

After the first couple hours, Dad taps at the window. "That's a mental hospital," he says.

I stare at an ominous institution of faded bricks, imagine all the suffering hiding behind those walls.

"If this drive is any longer, you'll have to drop me off there," he chuckles.

I let out a half-hearted laugh. *Now is a really interesting time to crack that joke, Dad.*

We stop at a coffee shop to get me a drink. They get my order wrong, and I burst into tears in the car. Two hundred disgusting calories in a cup, and the coffee doesn't even taste good. I picture all the suffering I had to go through to lose the calories that I am now choking down.

I pull myself together and go back inside to ask if they can fix it. The barista responds by dumping a vat of sugary, calorie-dense caramel syrup into it. I watch in horror. When I go back to the car to take a sip, it's cloying and overwhelmingly sweet. I'm so frustrated with myself; *It's just a fucking coffee, drink it,* I tell myself. It feels like such a ridiculous thing to be crying over, but I can't stop.

"Don't cry, love," my mom says sweetly. She heads in to get another coffee. "I'll watch them prepare it," she vows before she leaves. I sink into my seat as she talks to the barista. I hope the barista can't see me through the glass facade of the coffee shop. *She'll be thinking I'm a pain in the ass,* I think, trying to wipe up my tears so I don't upset my parents any more than I already have. I'm so ashamed.

From the passenger seat, Dad flips through radio stations. He lands on the nineties station—it's a song I don't recognize, the dark melody buried somewhere deep beneath rough guitar distortions and the gravelly voices of smokers. He nods his head along to the beat.

A while later, we stop for lunch, which thankfully goes better. We eat as we drive.

The sky is dark grey and heavy with clouds, promising rain. I open my window a crack and let the fresh, thick air blow my hair and rush into my lungs.

Outside, countryside fades into suburbia, which fades into the city centre. Stores, restaurants, houses, and apartments are crammed together — a dense cluster of life.

"Here we are," Mom says eventually as we approach a wide, towering building.

UNIVERSITY OF ALBERTA HOSPITAL

a sign out front reads. My heart is hammering.

I don't want to go inside.

Don't make me go inside.

Dread sits like a pit in my stomach.

Mom parks the car in the musty parkade building beside the hospital, and we walk over a covered glass bridge to get inside.

I trudge along, head down, hands shoved in my pockets. I don't want to raise my eyes above the tiled floor. I don't want to face this horrible place. I turn up the volume on my headphones to drown out the sound of my pounding heart.

We approach a woman behind a desk, hunched in front of a computer. A half-empty bottle of hand sanitizer sits before us; we each take a quick pump. "Could you tell us where the eating disorder unit is?" my mom asks. The woman quickly glances over at me, surveying me like some sort of rare species.

She points down a hall. "Just that way. Follow the signs."

We move onwards through the labyrinth of hallways. There are no windows here, and the blank walls feel claustrophobic. Arrowed signs guide the way.

Inside me, Ed and the Mysterious Girl hold their breaths. We push through a set of heavy-duty doors and into a waiting room.

It's a strange room, brutally outdated. The floor is coated in brown carpet, and the walls are a yellowish beige. Framed quotations hang on the wall – the stupid motivational ones that you would find in a second-grade classroom. Some chairs are pushed up in one corner of the room, and a hallway in the other corner delves deeper into the ward. Across from the chairs is a closed door.

I turn off the music in my headphones – an instinct inside me tells me that I need to be aware of my surroundings, on the lookout for danger.

My parents and I silently sit down in the chairs. Dad pulls out his phone and starts scrolling. No one says anything – there's nothing to say. All we can do is wait.

I feel my spine and ribs press against the back of the hard vinyl backing of the chair, and I wince at the pain.

My phone buzzes, and I slide it out of my pocket. Jade.

Good luck.

My frantic thoughts fill the silence of the room, shouting over each other. It's deafening. I put my head in my hands as I try to silence them all, but it's no use. Maybe their chaos is better than the deathly quiet.

A clock ticks in the corner of the room. It's one o'clock now. Nothing but seconds lie between me and the assessment.

The seconds bleed away.

Tick.

Tick.

Tick.

The quiet before the storm. I stare at the closed door on the other side of the room, my muscles tensed. My jaw clenched. I squeeze my left hand with my right, trying to think about the Mysterious Girl.

I just want to go home.

The creaking of the hinges breaks the silence. The door swings open.

A thin woman with glasses and grey hair stands in the doorway. She's wearing a pale blue medical mask; her eyes are cold and unreadable. I feel the weight of those blank eyes settling on me.

"Charlotte Bellows?"

My stomach drops. We stare at each other, but I don't answer her.

"Come on in," she says. Reluctantly, I stand. My parents stand up too, until she says, "Just Charlotte, for the start."

They sit back down. My mom gestures for me to take off my silent headphones, and extends a hand for me to place them in. I hand them over.

I pass through the doorway, leaving any last trace of security behind me. I'm in a large office with a PhD in psychiatry hanging on the wall. A man with dark brown eyes sits at a desk. Three chairs wait on my side of this desk.

"I'm Dr. Blunt," the woman says. She looks like Meryl Streep in *The Devil Wears Prada*. I shake her hand listlessly before she sits down beside the man at the desk. "This is our resident psychologist, Mr. Anderson," she introduces, gesturing to him.

"Hello," he says. "It's nice to meet you, Charlotte." Everything sounds so scripted.

I stare at him and nod.

Mr. Anderson asks me a variety of things he could search up on my medical file.

"How tall are you? Five-nine?"

"Five-eight."

"How much did you weigh before?"

Before Ed groomed his way into my life. Before he started starving me, slow and gradual at first, then quickly, forcefully. Before everything started falling apart.

What a loaded word — 'before.'

I don't want to think about how much I weighed before. I don't want to think about how my thighs pressed against each other when I sat down. The way my stomach folded when I bent over. I mumble the number, my eyes on the ugly carpeted floor.

"What's the lowest your weight has ever been?" he asks.

I tell them that, too. I know that's going to be used against me. As I say it, I don't know if I feel hopeless or proud that no one's been able to raise that number.

So far, this is shaping up to be a pretty great resumé for a hospital bed.

Dr. Blunt is scribbling something on a clipboard, which she shields from my view. I try to crane my neck to look at it, but I can't see whatever she's putting down.

Her phone is out on the desk, and it pings with a notification. She stops, picks it up, answers a text. I've driven three hours to attend this unpleasant appointment, and she's on her phone. I watch her coldly as Mr. Anderson continues the interrogation.

"Have you ever self-harmed?"

"No."

"Have you ever contemplated suicide?"

"Sure," I say, casually shifting my eyes back to the psychologist. "Sometimes." Ed is whispering to me from the dark alleyways of the Deep, even as I speak. Of things worse than death.

I don't mention that, though.

"Have you ever purged?" he asks.

"No."

Dr. Blunt puts down her phone in my peripheral vision.

"What are your thoughts on being hospitalized?"

Is this some sort of joke?

"I'm more scared of hospitalization than I am of death," Ed says flatly. Or is it me talking? I can barely tell anymore. We seem to be merging into one.

My palms are sweating. These strangers, trying to rip control away from me.

Mr. Anderson stares back at me for a moment, and I hold eye contact with him. His eyebrows crawl slightly up his forehead in surprise.

"We're going to call your parents in for the next part of the assessment." Soon my parents are sitting in the chairs next to me.

I watch Dr. Blunt as she sits back down. I look at the way her collarbones protrude from her shoulders, the thinness of her limbs, the way her torso suddenly curves in at her waistline. *My god, she is so thin.* She herself looks anorexic. An anorexic trying to steal *my* anorexia from me. I feel my cheeks warm with anger at the unfairness of it all.

I dig deeper into my cuticles. Little spots of blood appear. I keep digging.

"She'd be sharing a room with one other patient. In-hospital recovery usually takes about three months. Calorie intake varies depending on the patient, but we typically shoot for between thirty-two hundred and thirty-nine hundred," she explains.

'All our hard work, gone up in smoke,' Ed whispers. He sounds as panicked as I feel. *'You have model measurements. You are what everyone aspires to be. And they're going to take it all away.'*

I look around the room. I want to smash it all — I want to destroy it down to dust and splinters. I want to unleash the tornado that's been destroying my mind into this office, my fists like the powerful surges of wind, tearing and pounding relentlessly. I want Dr. Blunt to look at the ruined room and not even recognize it once was hers, just as I feel when I look in a mirror. *Show her what it's like show her what it's like show her what it's like.*

"We typically shoot for a BMI of twenty," Dr. Blunt explains.

Holy shit. Even before I started losing weight, my BMI was lower than that. They're going to make me even bigger than I was before. My vision begins to blur with tears.

There's no way her BMI is twenty. Hypocrite.

"We typically give patients the amount of calories they need to maintain in food, and then the rest in liquid meal replacement. Then, we just take out the liquid meal replacement when they're at their ideal weight. It makes for a very smooth transition," Dr. Blunt continues. She's not speaking to me at all, only to my parents. It's what could potentially be the biggest change in my life, and she's not even including me. She's stealing away every last bit of control like I'm invisible, not even in the room.

My parents are nodding, and my mom is writing in a notebook that she's brought. Dad stays quiet. Mom begins asking Dr. Blunt questions, but I can't hear them. My thoughts are too loud.

This can't be real. This can't be happening.

I glue my eyes to the floor beneath my feet as the tears begin to roll down my face.

Then, cold, bony fingers rest on my shoulder from behind. '*I see you,*' a low, raspy voice says. The hand gently squeezes my shoulder. '*I see that you're trying. You're in constant search of some sort of hope in all the pain,*' Ed continues. '*But pain, you're discovering, is a very dark thing.*'

He's the enemy, but he's all I have. I want to turn around and hug Ed so badly, let his warm and secure hold seep comfort into me. I want him to be the Ed that cares about me.

'*Just look at what a miserable thing this is.*' Ed leans in close beside my ear. '*This suffering is brutal to the point of being inhumane. There's nothing salvageable left in this mess. Spare yourself.*'

My tears drip down my neck, leaving cold wet trails

on my skin. Ed reaches around and wipes them from my face. 'Oh, Charlotte,' he sighs. '*Where did it all go so wrong?*'

There's this dark cloud inside me. It follows me everywhere. I can't tell if it's Ed or the very essence that Ed is trying to protect me from.

It distorts my perception.

It makes truths sound like lies.

I inhale it, bringing it in deeper.

Deeper.

Deeper.

While my parents' mouths keep moving, while my life is being planned.

RAIN

"*Thanks for coming.* We'll keep in touch," Dr. Blunt says. To her, I'm just another name on a long list. Shakily, I stand up.

Everything around me distorted and unreal. I don't feel connected to my body — it's like I'm watching all these things happen to me without feeling a thing.

I've been tied down to earth by a string, and the string has finally been ripped in two. Now, I'm aimlessly floating through space. Lost.

I burst through the ward door and begin gaining speed. My footsteps echo in the hallway, coming back at me from all different directions.

I start running.

Nothing matters anymore, I just have to get away.

"Charlotte!" my mom shouts after me.

I don't stop.

I don't even look back.

I pump my legs faster and faster. The walls of the hospital hallway blurring past me.

Hospitalization — this can't be happening. This can't be real.

My eyes are burning.

I fly past the secretary at the front desk, who barely has time to look up. My lungs are burning, but I only push harder. I stumble through the door to the parkade, going so fast my legs can barely carry me.

Tears streaming from my face, mucus leaking from my nose, my entire face is an ocean of crashing waves. I taste salt.

I'm out on an empty street.

Rain crashes down, exploding against the sidewalk. It drips down my neck, down my back. If I close my eyes, it would feel like I'm caught in the dark, viciously windy funnel of a tornado.

I don't close my eyes, though. I stare into this storm. I see it for the terrifying, annihilating danger that it is; I face it with all the fortitude I have—because what have I got left to lose?

I keep moving, trying to outrun something I know isn't outrunable.

My feet strike puddles, causing water to splash up to the knees of my pants.

I run faster, faster, faster.

I throw my head in the air and scream. A horrible, animalistic sound, loaded with anguish and suffering and shame and loneliness, rips through the air. All the pain of the last months, flooding out into the wet air, blending with the raindrops and crashing down on me. I'm drowning in it. It echoes off the buildings, as if the world is screaming back at me.

Something inside of me has finally burst; I scream with all my built-up rage against the world.

I scream at Ana, for turning on me so suddenly, and messing with my friendship with Jade like it was some sort of game.

I scream at my parents for the way they unassumingly kindled unhealthy ideas.

I scream at society for telling me to lose just a little more weight to be pretty until there was nothing left but skin and bones, nothing left to lose but life itself.

I scream at Dr. Vernon, who should've recognized what was happening earlier on, who should've come to save me from Ed, but did nothing.

I scream at my own mind, for doing such a horrible, cruel thing to my body.

My hair is sticking to the sides of my face. My wet clothes hanging from my body. I sob as I run, a convulsive and violent gasping. The rain washes my tears from my cheeks.

My sides are burning with cramps. I collapse to the ground, dry heaving. I see my reflection in the pools of water by the side of the road, and I smash it with my hands, destroying the image of a lost little girl with thrashing ripples of water.

Exhausted, I succumb to reality, unable to get back up. I lie on the pavement, curled up, my eyes squeezed tightly shut. The rain lashes me, soaking my clothes, and streaking down me. I'm melting into the ground.

I stay there, shivering, and let the rain wash me pure; I let it wash me of all this bottled-up rage.

love

/ləv/

noun

1. an intense feeling of deep affection.

MESSY, INCOHERENT THINGS

When I get home, I run upstairs, lock myself in my bedroom, and collapse on to my bed. For a moment, I just lie there with my eyes closed.

I feel my phone buzz in my pocket. I pull it out. A message from Jade:

How did things end up?

I explain the disaster that was the trip to the University of Alberta Hospital.

She listens (or reads, more accurately, I guess). She doesn't try to encourage me, because I've already heard all the encouragement there is to hear, and I think Jade knows that. She also doesn't try to look on the bright side, because let's face it, there isn't one. She keeps me company, and agrees. Yes. This sucks.

There's something relieving about how raw and honest our conversation is.

She's a little section of my life reserved for nothing but the truth — a section where I don't have to put on a brave face to minimize any collateral damage, or try to articulate words that are meant to be messy and incoherent by nature. She's been there before, in her own unique way. She understands.

And then there's Mom.

MOM

Sometimes, I look at my mom and try to ingrain every little detail of her into my memory. When we watch TV together, I occasionally glance over at her instead of the screen: the gold ring around each of her pupils, followed by deep greenish hazel. The way those pupils swiftly flick around as she takes in whatever's happening. The way her dark eyelashes swoop out from her lash line, quickly coming together as she blinks before opening again. The way the corners of her narrow lips turn upwards when something funny happens. Even resting, her face is life in motion.

Home.

This old house has seen a lot. Strange sounds of memory echo through empty hallways and bloom in vacant rooms. I know that one day, in weeks or years, I'll feel nostalgic for this moment — when Mom, Dad, Parker, and I were together, under the same roof.

When I finish high school — university. Or even in weeks — the hospital.

Me, in an unrecognizable place with unrecognizable people.

I'm going to have to part ways, go off on my own, eventually. I try to imagine myself making only one cup of coffee in the morning, instead of an entire pot for four.

A long beep throughout a sleepy house — the coffee machine, finished brewing.

A timid creaking of a door hinge.

The warmth of a smile.

NIGHTTIME THOUGHTS

If there's ever been a motivation to eat more, this is it.

My hatred for Dr. Blunt haunts me like a ghost. It follows me back to Calgary and stays with me throughout each day. I don't want to be held captive at the hospital.

Nor do I want to be held captive in Ed's basement.

So I choke down each snack and meal and ride out the horrible guilt that comes directly after.

"What are you gonna have for your evening snack?" Parker asks at night. With grass-stained khakis and dishevelled hair, he has a wild look about him after his day at school. Parker asks this every night, so he can join in — he's always had a sweet tooth.

I look up from the homework I'm working on in the dining room. "Ice cream, I was thinking? What are you in the mood for?"

"Ice cream sounds good!" he says, eyes gleaming with excitement.

"I could go for some right now, actually — are you hungry?" I ask.

He smiles. "I've gotchu."

He runs to the kitchen to get the carton from the freezer; I jump up and chase after him.

We sit across from each other at the table as we eat, chatting. I listen to Parker's animated voice and try to ignore the cramping feeling of guilt as I raise the spoon to my mouth. Rich chocolate flavour melts on my tongue. Our conversation acts as a decent distraction.

Dr. Blunt will be keeping a close watch on me to see how the next couple of weeks go, as we wait for a bed to come up in the ward. Nothing is off the table.

Bravery is not in the act of winning, I learn, but rather in the act of fighting. Maybe it's even braver fighting a battle you know you might very well lose.

When I next wake up in the Deep, I head outside. I walk through the meadow and to the oak tree. The Mysterious Girl isn't there, but I still climb up the branches and sit on the lowest one. I look through the canopy of leaves at the stars above.

"Are you close?" I hear a voice ask. I look down to see the Mysterious Girl looking back up at me from the ground.

"Close to what?" I say, confused.

"Close to finding out who I am," she answers.

I stare at her for a long time. Then, something occurs to me. "Are you me?"

"I am you, and you are me." She nods.

I squint up at the sky as I think about that for a moment. "So I guess the real question is: who am I?"

"I guess you'll have to find out," the Mysterious Girl says with a smile, and she begins walking back to the townsite, leaving me with the company of my thoughts and the stars.

BITTERSWEET

The weigh-in is just as intense as it's always been. My mom chews her lips absentmindedly in the car as we listen to the radio. I pick at my nails.

As we walk into the doctor's office, I know that Edmonton is watching. The office is still and empty, as if the room itself is holding its breath in anticipation.

"Charlotte Bellows," I tell the medical assistant working at the front desk.

She types into her computer, then gets up and says, "You know the drill."

I kick off my shoes and take off my jacket, handing it to Mom.

I pass by the desk to the corner of the room, where I turn around and step back onto the scale.

For the first time, I find myself hoping I've gained. *Please*, I think desperately.

We live in a world where a number on a scale can determine whether an entire week was a success or not. It's a scale—stainless steel and some metal springs. What a crazy thing to let control your life.

"You can get off now," the medical assistant tells me.

I step off, put my shoes back on, and take my jacket back from my mom. The medical assistant turns to her computer, and I can hear the printer whizzing to life. It spits out a sheet of paper, which the medical assistant takes and folds closed.

She hands it to my mom, who immediately unfolds it.

It's a blind weigh-in, so I'm not supposed to know if I've gained or lost weight, but I can read my mom for a reaction.

Her eyes light up, and the faintest of smiles tugs at the corners of her lips before she forces down any trace of expression and becomes unreadable.

I'm not sure if that reaction makes me happy or sad.

Maybe a little of both.

THE MIRROR

Parker and I continue to have our evening snacks together. The flavours — the subtle bitterness of dark chocolate, the creaminess of ice cream, the sweetness of salted caramel — start to grow on me. It's been a while since I've actually enjoyed food.

A sharp aching in my lower abdomen ends up being my period. "Rejoice," I mutter, rolling my eyes as I plop an Advil into my mouth.

Michelle is thrilled when I tell her — at our next session, she gives me a dark, shiny stone in a little silk pocket. I slide it out for further examination; it's covered in faint splotches of red.

"It's bloodstone," Michelle adds excitedly. "To symbolize this important milestone."

Her enthusiasm is not shared. Still, it's a sweet — if not slightly strange — gesture.

I smile. "Thank you!"

Weeks later, I stand in front of my mirror and stare at the girl who is staring back.

She doesn't look the same as she used to.

Where there used to be the sharp ridges of bones, there are smoother, softer curves. I lightly trace my torso with my hand. My ribs have disappeared beneath my skin.

Part of me longs for them, and misses the way they used to feel beneath my fingers. I can tell Ed is stunned. He's mourning the loss of my extreme thinness.

If I raise my eyes, though, my cheeks glow with a faint pink hue, and my eyes sparkle the way the Mysterious Girl's eyes did the night we went stargazing. Life is slowly but surely flowing back into me.

I look less like Ed and more like the Mysterious Girl. This is me.

There's a tinge of relief, a tenseness in my chest gradually relaxing — putting the countless hospital trips further behind me. More distance between me and death. There's a future out there that I'll be alive for.

Instinctively, I stretch my finger and thumb around my wrist. Despite the weight I've gained back, they still touch. Something that I told myself determined my thinness was actually just my bone structure; I didn't have control over it either way. *Huh.* I wonder what else I've tricked myself into believing.

I look back down at my changed body.

But the longer I stare at my reflection, the more I notice. The width of my waist. The subtle but present traces of cellulite along the tops of my hamstrings. Are those faint stretch marks on my inner thighs? Sometimes, it feels like my thin body was all I had going for me. What am I without it?

Who could ever love me like this?

I know gaining weight is supposed to be good news, so why does part of me still feel so awful?

There's a deep aching alongside the relief, a longing for the way things were before. So much flesh on my body that doesn't feel like my own. My bones are trapped beneath a layer of fat that shouldn't be there. I'm burying my beauty in it, to the point people can barely see the elegance anymore. I'm putting more distance between me and Ed.

Carefully, I lower the mirror off the wall. Turning it sideways, I grab it beneath my arm. Heedful not to hit any walls with it, I carry it out of my bedroom and through the house, down into the basement.

I squint through the darkness as I reach the bottom of the stairs, and prop the mirror against the wall.

This will be its new home, far away from the rest of the house.

In the sparse light, I see the faint outline of my face peeking through the darkness.

From the hard coldness in this reflection's eyes, I can tell it's Ed. There's an eerie threatening in his wide, blank eyes.

For a second, I'm held captive in his stare.

He's disappointed in me for beginning to give in to all the people who've been trying to separate us for so long.

He's disgusted at me for gaining weight.

He's enraged at me for not listening to him.

'It's not too late,' he whispers. '*It's not too late to go back to the perfection we were before.*'

I turn around and sprint up the stairs as fast as I can, my feet thudding on each step.

LEVITATING

There's an impish look in Olivia's eyes this Saturday night, sprawled across my basement couch. We're watching TV — she glances sideways at me, then back to the screen; back at me again. She's been much more cheerful recently — the cruelty at school seems to have lost its grasp on her, at least for now, as if there's an end in sight. I wonder what's changed.

"What is it?" I ask, narrowing my eyes and grinning. She doesn't answer at first; I playfully push her knee. "Tell me!"

She reaches for the remote. Pauses the movie we're watching. "How's your blood pressure doing?" she asks with a strange eagerness.

"*That's* what you were thinking about?" I groan, rolling my eyes and smiling. "I was out here preparing for a scandal." She keeps staring at me — when I realize she's waiting for an answer, I add, seriously, "It's good, though. A lot better than before." My mom had told me about the rise in my blood pressure after our last check-in, desperate to confide her relief.

"So, if it by chance dropped a little . . . You wouldn't die on me?"

"Why would it be dropping?" I ask.

"Well, I read that when you smoke weed —"

"No way!"

"Yes way!" She's smiling from ear to ear.

"How did you get it?"

"A sketchy online website," she says. "I was lowkey worried they would take my credit card information and dip, but I mean, I got the weed."

I shrug. "They delivered."

"It's a dab pen," she says as she springs from the couch and roots through her backpack on the floor. Her eyes are radiant as she pulls out a small, narrow package. "Behold."

I slide down onto the floor and squint at it. There's an image of an unkempt man on the box — long, dark brown hair, goatee. "Is that . . ."

"Jack Sparrow, from *Pirates of the Caribbean*," Olivia says. "Weird, I know. But it was this or a half-naked woman."

Jack Sparrow stares at me, dark circles beneath his judgmental eyes.

I pause for a moment. "You know . . ." I say. "My parents have vodka in the freezer, if we feel like going really wild." I would never have done this a couple months ago — the liquid calories would've been too much to handle. *Fuck it.* I can't keep depriving myself from new experiences.

"Are you suggesting getting crossed?" Olivia asks.

I nod.

"I'm in."

That's how we find ourselves slipping out the front door at two in the morning. A backpack is slung over my shoulders, weighted with the bottle of alcohol, along with the dab pen.

Winter has lost its icy grasp on the temperature; it's fresh, dewy — spring.

Finally.

Buzzing with anticipation, we race through the streets.

"Where are we going?" Olivia asks.

"The university. I think I know a spot."

Several blocks later, we arrive at Mount Royal University, a small campus planted in the middle of a mostly residential area. It's completely quiet, just me and Olivia, our breathing and laughter. We run, run, run through the lush green soccer fields on the outskirts of the grounds.

We reach an empty parkade. "Through here," I say, sliding into the car entrance. The smell of gasoline hangs in the air. Streetlights from outside cast long shadows throughout the dim parking level. Our shadows, stretched and contorted, sprint to the stairs with sweeping legs.

We thud up the stairwell, footsteps echoing. By the time we burst through the door at the top level, we're out of breath. I look at the expansive sky spreading out above us. Several kilometres away, downtown sparkles with lights, impressive skyscrapers bursting from the ground with a navy glow.

I slide the backpack off my shoulders and put it down at my feet; unzip it.

"What first?" I ask.

Olivia peers into the bag. "Vodka?"

The bottle shines as I pull it out, crystal-clear liquid sloshing around.

I pause. "Shoot."

"What?"

"We forgot shot glasses," I say.

Olivia shrugs nonchalantly. "We can just drink it from the bottle."

I stare at her. "Hardcore." Unscrew the cap.

The rim of the bottle is cold against my lips as I chug it back. The pungent flavour floods my mouth; the muscles in my throat tense up, unwilling to let the foul taste go any further. I force it down, leaving a trail of bitter tang and warmth.

Then it hits my stomach.

Heat, blooming. Seeping through my blood.

I blink. "Whoa."

"Are you gonna throw up?" Olivia asks nervously.

"No, I'm not gonna throw up," I laugh.

"What does it taste like?"

"Like . . . a hug from the inside?"

She raises her eyebrows.

"Okay, it tastes like shit," I say. "But it feels nice." I pass her the bottle.

She grips its smooth neck and chugs it back. She recoils, and her face scrunches up.

"Oh my god," she says after swallowing it, shaking her head.

Then she stops. Looks at the sky. Smiles. "I get what you mean, though. A hug from the inside."

We pass the bottle back and forth a few more times. The warm feeling intensifies, spreads. Olivia's cheeks flush. A pleasant fog settles over my mind. The heat of the vodka. The cool of the night. Like the spring equinox — perfect balance.

"Weed?" Olivia suggests.

"Weed," I agree, putting the vodka back in the bag and pulling out the dab pen. "Your turn to go first." I pass it to her.

She stops, examines the picture of Jack a final time. "How deep do I inhale?" she asks, pulling the pen out of the box.

"Um . . . as deep as you can?" *Go big or go home.*

She nestles the pen between her lips. Breathes in. I watch the smoke curl from her mouth; escape her nostrils.

It rises up in a sharp-smelling haze. We watch it disappear into the air, hypnotized.

Olivia buries her face in her arm and coughs.

"You good?" I ask. My voice sounds strange and foreign — *Is that really what I sound like?*

She nods and extends the pen with an open hand. I lift it, cool and smooth beneath my fingers. Inhale.

The back of my throat burns with sweet, chemical citrus.

I cough, too. When the searing, itching sensation leaves my throat, I say, "Is this thing flavoured?" I read the label. "*Sorbet.*"

"That is *not* sorbet."

"At least it doesn't taste like skunk."

"True. Can I have another hit?"

I give Jack back to her, and wander over to the edge of the parkade. Olivia follows me — I hear her inhale and exhale again behind me. I rest my forearms against the concrete border and lean forwards. A fifty-foot drop beneath me. I look back up. The city sparkles. The moon glows.

"It's pretty," Olivia says softly.

I look at her — the gentleness of her relaxed features. *Do you feel peaceful? Happy?*

This is all I know of peace — all I know of happiness.

I take Jack back for another hit. We pass him back and forth, drawing in with greedy lungs.

Three hits each.

Four.

Five.

I float up into the air — a cloud. I giggle.

"What is it?" Olivia asks, giggling now too.

"Nothing," I say, smiling and shaking my head. "I'm just really fucking happy right now." Calm. Giddy. Simply content.

Olivia's brown eyes are glassy. In the distance, the city lights are brighter, more colourful.

Somewhere below — hissing. Sprinklers are shooting water in the green fields.

"Let's go!" Olivia says, and takes off running towards the exit.

I take one more quick hit and throw Jack in the backpack. "Wait up!" I call, clumsily zipping it up. Clunky fingers. *Holy shit, my hands are* HUGE. I giggle some more.

We stumble down the stairwell and back through the parkade.

The world is spinning; Olivia moves in sudden, streaking blurs. I feel water soak through my Converse shoes as I step onto the grass. *Squelch.*

The soft spray of water catches the moonlight and sparkles as it flows around me. We sprint in circles around the sprinklers, ducking, jumping, laughing. Enveloped in cool mist.

Olivia stops and faces the water; it condenses on her face and rolls from her cheeks. Her eyeliner drips in murky black streaks. I stick my tongue out, feel traces of water dampen my mouth. My clothes hang to my body — chilly, but I don't mind. The warmth of the vodka courses through me. *Wait — the vodka! I forgot!*

I plop down on the wet grass and pull out the bottle. Olivia sits across from me, eyeballing the alcohol excitedly. I throw my head back and drown myself in it. Is it dribbling down my chin? Or is that just the water?

The darkness of the night feels like the darkness of my eyelids — like I'm all imagining this ethereal night, a warm, hazy dream with the soft, pulsing glow in the streetlights, in the moon, in Olivia's eyes.

Levitating.

I hand it to Olivia. She takes a hearty gulp; puts it down. Her hair is plastered to the sides of her face.

The water around us shimmers brighter, closing us off from the rest of the world.

Her and me.

It's always going to be her and me.

I grab her wet face; she grabs mine. Breathless, laughing.

"You're beautiful, Charlotte," she says.

"We're immortal, Olivia," I laugh. "You know that, don't you? We're fucking immortal."

Olivia smiles, her smeared eyes scrunching up.

THE MONSTER AND ME

A *couple nights later*, I sit on a curb by the side of the road in the Deep. It's a calm night, and the cool breeze blows gently through my hair. The street is basked in pale moonlight, and the air feels fresh and clear in my lungs; I take a deep breath, I kick absentmindedly at the small pebbles along the edge of the dirt road, and try to ignore the pleading inside of me, begging me to go find Ed.

It turns out I don't have to. He's already found me. His gentle footsteps make me turn.

I look up at his narrow, pale face.

The Mysterious Girl can only protect me if I have it in me to protect myself. And I'm trying, I really am, but nothing seems to make him go away. I hate to admit it, but part of me is glad he's here. I like his company.

"May I sit?" he asks.

I don't answer. I put my chin in my hands and stare at my feet.

He sits down anyway, slowly adjusting himself next to me. I can tell from the slight grimace on his face when I glance over that the ground is hard against his exposed tailbone. We sit there like two old friends. We share the silence.

I know he sits with me, keeping me company during the darkest of times.

Is it worse to be hurt by your company, or to be utterly alone? The warmth, the comfort of unwavering companionship. Is occasional suffering a small price to pay for something so valuable?

I know Ed will never abandon me. I know he'll always be there for me. But he doesn't want the best for me. After the basement, I know how badly he'll hurt me, how far he'll go.

Finally, I break the silence. "I'm not supposed to be friends with monsters," I say softly.

So hard to say. But I want Ed, the healthy, happy friend he was before things got serious — the one who exercised with me, the one who fuelled my body with nutritious foods.

Before I became medically unstable.

Before I started dying.

Before — everything.

"What makes me a monster?" he asks, voice just as soft as mine. He sounds hurt — like after all this, he still doesn't know what he's done to me.

"You tried to kill me," I say. My eyes warm with tears. I keep them glued to the ground ahead of me. I don't want to look at his face. If I do, I might never be able to look away again.

"No, you tried to kill yourself," he says empathetically. "I merely kept you company throughout the suffering." When I don't answer, he adds, "I was there for you."

"I don't want to talk to you anymore," I murmur. A tear rolls down the side of my face, and Ed moves to dab it from my cheek, but I brush him away.

"Who else do you have to talk to?" he asks sadly. "I'm all you have."

He's not all that I have. I have my parents. I have

Parker. I have Jade. I have Olivia. But will they ever be able to understand me at the level that Ed does? Sometimes, I just don't think it's possible. It's like he and I were made for each other. Our destinies meant to be intertwined.

I miss him. I don't want to admit it, but there isn't a day that passes without me thinking of him. More tears trail down my face. I don't want to say goodbye. I never want to say goodbye.

"Go," I whisper, my voice quavering.

I think Ed knows how much I miss him. How much I want to come running back to his comfort. And I'm certain he thinks I will, because he slowly stands, his frail joints creaking.

He sighs dismally. "You know where to find me," he says. "I'll be waiting for you, Charlotte."

It takes everything I have not to run after him as he walks away into the night, disappearing into the shadows. It might've been the hardest thing I ever did. My eyes burn with tears; the morning can't come fast enough.

FLIGHT

The first rays of the rising sun are beginning to streak across the city when my phone vibrates. It's a notification from Olivia:

I'm out back!

I grab some house keys from the kitchen counter and shove them into my pocket before bursting out the back door. I'm immediately greeted with a rush of fresh air, sweet with the smell of mowed grass. The sun bathes me in its warm, golden light. I run to the garage and carefully guide my bicycle out into the alleyway, where Olivia is waiting.

After the progress I've made, I've finally been allowed to bike to school again — just in time for the pleasant spring weather.

"What a beautiful morning!" I exclaim.

"I know, right?"

We jump on our bikes and take off down the alleyway, riding beside each other as we chat about the day ahead of us. We pedal over lush, green grass to get to the sidewalk; from there on, I lead the way.

My bike glides over the pavement as I pump my legs with power and energy. I'm gaining speed, moving faster and faster.

"Wait up!" Olivia calls from behind.

I'm blasting up the hill between us and school, like a plane speeding down a runway. My hair blowing back from my face. I find myself grinning eagerly as I approach the top.

And there it is — that moment of satisfaction when I reach the summit of the hill. I look up. What a beautiful view of the city from here — I can see right over the houses to the shining skyscrapers of downtown. They sparkle in the reflecting sunlight.

My momentum drifts me over the peak of the hill, and — a race down the other side! The sidewalk is a blur beneath my tires. Thrill rushes through my chest at the speed. I laugh in spite of myself. Moving so quickly feels so freeing, like I'm finally breaking free of whatever invisible restraints had been holding me back.

I stand up on the pedals, stretching out my legs. Then, I lean forward over the handlebars, just slightly, so that I can't see the bike beneath me. I raise my head to the sky and feel the wind cascade across my face.

I'm taking flight.

AN ABUNDANCE
OF NUMBERS

I'm sitting in math class, trying not to eavesdrop on the boys slouched across from me as we wait for the teacher to start the lesson. Is it really eavesdropping if they're right there? It's not like I can turn my ears off . . .

"You free this weekend? The boys are coming over to my house on Saturday," one boy says. So much gel in his hair! It could probably serve him as a helmet.

"Sorry, can't. My sister's in town for the weekend," the other kid answers, shaking his head with a frown. I'm pretty sure his name is Patrick. I've had a few other classes with him. There's an open bag of Doritos on his desk, and he reaches in and pops a chip into his mouth absentmindedly. His chewing is loud and crunchy.

"Ooo, you have a sister?" the first boy says. I glance over just in time to see his eyebrows wiggle suggestively.

"Nah, dude, she's fat," Patrick says.

What the fuck?

At the front of the class, the teacher starts talking, and the chatter of the class dies away — but not the bitter aftertaste of Patrick's words.

Later that day, I'm sitting in social studies, slumped over on my desk — drowsy and bored, warily watching the teacher speak in front of a projector screen at the front of the class. I know I should be paying closer attention, and something catches my eye — the girl at the desk one over from me has small printing scrawled across the palm of her left hand with ink.

I peer at it.

Tea — 30
Smoothie — 200
Wrap — 400

There's no way to un-see it. It's the food she's eaten today, next to its caloric density.

'Why can't you just be like her?' Ed whispers bitterly.

A surprise flood of sadness for this girl. Food was never meant to be tracked this closely. Teenage girls should live life beyond nutritional information — everyone should. There's so much more to life than numbers.

Eating 'healthy' can turn into an unhealthy obsession, and it looks like this kid's in the midst of crossing a line. Details as subtle as ink on a hand don't tell everything about what a person is going through, but they sure can be a good indicator.

I imagine myself into her head.

She stares at her own body in the mirror, desperately wishing it would shrink.

She shares her mind with a powerful, malevolent force — her own version of Ed.

I don't know this girl at all. Should I say something, anyway? What would I even say? Before I can decide what to do, she lowers her hand into her lap, and the writing disappears from my view.

I feel an ache of worry and empathy. Don't follow him, I think to her.

The bell rings, and everyone stands up and gathers their things to go. I rise to my feet, slinging my backpack over my shoulder, and watch as all the other students stream out of the room. My mind is a flurry of questions.

How many more girls are struggling with this?

How common is it?

This disease exists beyond just me. It exists every-where — a horrible parasite that is nurtured with adver-tisements, models, diet and clothing companies, the male gaze . . . everything.

How do you save girls from daily living?

A PHONE CALL

That evening, we're having dinner — Dad's steak, with Caesar salad — when my mom's phone rings. She puts down her cutlery and whips her phone out of her pocket. "Dr. Blunt," she says with a frown. "I'll be right back." And she rushes upstairs to answer the call.

Dad, Parker, and I wait in anxious silence for her to return.

A dawning sense of dread. *This could be it — they could have an open bed. I'll get shipped away.*

I've made progress, but have I made enough?

Dad reaches his hand across the table and puts it on top of mine.

Parker's eyes glisten, stunned by fear. He's holding his breath.

After what feels like an eternity, Mom returns to the living room. There's a broad smile on her face. "Dr. Blunt is happy with your progress over the past couple weeks," she announces. "You aren't off the hook yet, but if we can keep up the good work, there's a chance you might be able to stay at home."

I can hardly believe it.

Finally, my struggling is paying off.

I jump out of my chair and run into Mom's arms. She hugs me tightly. Dad gets up and puts his arm around the two of us. Parker nestles into the group hug.

It hadn't really crossed my mind before, but at this moment, it does: I forgive my parents. My mom shouldn't have brought me along for her diet and then criticized me when I got stressed around food. My dad shouldn't have made those comments on other people's bodies, especially when I was in recovery. I've understood their role for a while.

They may have helped raise Ed, but they raised me, too. They never intended for things to escalate like they did. I know they love me.

In this moment, everything is okay.

For now.

But maybe, just maybe, now is all I need.

Forgiveness.

When I was younger, I thought my parents were like gods — all-knowing, ever-powerful, the ultimate protection. But now that I've gotten older, I see that they're people, just like everyone else — people capable of love and mistakes.

PURPOSE

The night of the phone call, I pull out my phone and open a contact I haven't texted in a while — not since that rainy day in Edmonton, when it felt like the whole world was crashing down. A lot sure has changed since then.

Jade —

I wonder if events are predetermined. Maybe we were meant to meet years ago, but not for the purpose of being in a relationship. Maybe everything that happened had a reason, and this is it. Maybe everything led up to that cold night at the bus stop, where I knew I wasn't alone.

I dodged the hospital :)

NICE!!!

I'm so proud of you!!

I wonder if she knows the role she played in that.

THIS ISN'T A GOODBYE, IS IT?

"**I've been meaning** to tell you something," Olivia says.

It's a peaceful spring day, the sun peeking out from behind the clouds in warm rays. We're sitting on a bench on 17th Ave, spending lunch break together as usual. Pedestrians walk past us, carrying shopping bags, talking on phones. City life.

"Yeah?" I take a bite of my sandwich.

Her eyebrows knit together, and she brushes a strand of hair behind her ear; watches the cars pass by on the road. "I'm leaving."

I stare at her, confused. "Leaving what?"

"Western."

I put down my food. "Oh." My voice is quiet.

Silence. A car horn honks. A bird caws.

I should've seen it coming, but I'm still surprised. Dread churns in my stomach.

"Where are you going?" I ask.

"Central Memorial." She looks at me. "You know, that one near your house, by Crowchild Trail? I won't be too far."

I nod. I've passed by it many times before. "You think you'll like it there?"

"Yeah. I talked with the principal there and went on a little tour around the school. I think it's gonna be a really great program for me." She plops a Goldfish in her mouth from a plastic bag in her lap.

A *fresh start.*

I imagine her finding new friends, and me fighting for a space in her new crowded schedule. Something in my chest clenches. I glance back at Western, down the street. For the majority of the year, I've been too focused on surviving to make any new friends. It's always been the two of us, together.

I muster a smile. "I'm happy for you. You deserve a good high school experience."

She smiles at me, eyes scrunching up. The way she did on the bus ride to Michaels at the beginning of the year. The way she did beneath the sprinklers late that night. "Thanks."

"So, when are you going?"

"Next week."

"Oh. Wow." I stare at my shoes. The air feels colder. "That's soon."

"Yeah, it's the earliest admin could get me in."

She really is in a rush to get out of here. I look up at her. "This isn't a goodbye, is it?"

"God, no, Charlotte," she says, eyes soft with empathy. "We'll still hang out lots, I promise."

"Good," I say. Smiling. Biting the inside of my cheek. "I can't afford to lose my original partner in crime."

BEAUTY BEFORE

I'm scrolling through my Pinterest, looking to be inspired by any sort of art I can find, when I come across Renaissance sculptures. I notice something right away: these sculptures of women aren't stick thin. In fact, they look quite healthy.

There's one called Crouching Venus, by Doidalsa, where the goddess Venus is crouching down, her relaxed stomach folding. It's a famous, beautiful sculpture, well-known and admired. The Crouching Venus is priceless, and no one gives a shit about her size.

I continue my searching, diving deep into the internet. I find the Rubenesque era, which took place in the seventeenth century. The women portrayed in paintings then were full-figured, curvy, and shapely. Though society's definition of beautiful is strict and firm in the moment, it's been malleable over time.

'Beautiful' meant a very different thing back then. So where did everything change for the worse?

I'M OKAY

"*What are you thinking about for* your evening snack?" Parker asks. We're on the couch, having just finished watching a ridiculous scary movie spoof. My ribs are sore from laughing so hard.

"Chocolate, maybe?" I say as the credits fly past on the screen.

"Sounds delicious," he says, heading to the pantry. He returns with a box of chocolates and places it on the coffee table in front of me.

"Parker?"

"Yeah?"

"You don't have to eat if you're not hungry. I'm okay."

A quiet smile. He picks up his manga and sits down to read.

PARTING

That Friday, I walk out of the Western doors with Olivia for the last time.

"Well, this is it." She exhales, a look of relief in her eyes. "The end of an era."

"Your next era is gonna be a great one," I assure her.

We stroll to the bus stop. Soon, the bus rounds the corner and screeches to a halt in front of us. "Time to bust outta this hellhole," she whispers with a grin as we step on.

I try to ignore the drop of lonely disappointment — the plan had been to bust out of here side by side, diplomas in hand.

"I'm nervous for Central," she admits when we're seated.

"I hear they have a good art program — I'm sure that'll be fun."

"Yeah. It's just meeting new people." She puts her head back and stares at the bus's roof.

"Change isn't always comfortable," I say, thinking about how I'm leaving Ed. "But it's how you'll grow, right?"

She looks at me. Smiles. "That's true."

I fish my headphones out of my bag, plug them into my phone, and pass one earbud to Olivia. I try to soak up her presence as much as I can.

I don't want this bus ride to stop, don't want her to leave.

Eventually, though, the bus pulls up to her stop. Olivia stands up, steps out into the aisle.

"Good luck," I say. "You'll have to let me know how it goes."

"I will." She starts walking towards the open doors, but turns around for a moment. "See ya, Charlotte."

hope

/hōp/

verb

1. A belief that something could happen.

A FAMILIAR VOICE

One night, I'm venturing through the streets of the townsite in the Deep. I've been trying to learn the way all of the streets and alleyways and paths connect. There's a lot to discover. It's so peaceful here at nighttime.

"Charlotte!" a raspy voice calls.

I glance over to see Ed leaning against the facade of a house, arms crossed. He has a vain grin on his ghastly face.

I keep walking.

"Charlotte!" he repeats, this time with an edge of frustration in his voice.

I don't even look over my shoulder at him.

"This won't be the end of things!" he barks. "I won't leave you alone! Do you hear me, Charlotte?" His voice echoes off the buildings, down the streets and deep into my mind.

Stop being so loud!

I keep moving, leaving him behind.

It's *my* mind, not his. I can't forget—he was never my friend. He was my captor.

THE MEDIA

It's crazy, all the bullshit that the media will feed you. It's even crazier that you don't even consider it bullshit.

Michelle and I spend a session examining clothing advertisements together.

"This is Photoshopped," she tells me when I show her a Victoria's Secret ad.

"How do you know?" I ask.

"Well, first of all, these models are starving themselves," she states. "But look at this." She points to the legs of the models. "You see how it's shaded along the outer sides of the legs?"

I nod.

"Legs literally aren't that shape. Normally, it would be shaded along the insides."

"So why did they change it?"

"To make them look thinner," she explains. "There's more than just that. Photo editors pinch in the shoulders and the waists of women. They change close to everything."

Even most mannequins have unrealistic proportions. There is an entire industry out there, trying to profit off our insecurities.

Society's current definition of beauty isn't even human.

Thin to the point where it's literally ruining your life, and still it's what models strive for. Hair turning brittle and falling out. Menstrual cycles, the very thing that gives life, shutting down. Obsessing over food, letting fear of gaining weight control lives — but we're willing to look over all of that just to see a thigh gap and a flat stomach.

That's not beauty. That's suffering.

Later, as I wait outside for my dad to pick me up, I'm still thinking about how absurd and disturbing that truth is. Society believes that 'skinny' and 'beautiful' are automatic synonyms. People deprive themselves of natural, healthy bodies in a desperate attempt to mutilate their bodies into objects of skin and bone. The body's one job is to be a vessel for human life, yet society and diet culture support the idea of making that job harder, if not impossible.

I'm still thinking about it the next morning at breakfast, as I eat my granola.

I continue to think about it all week.

Skinny. We're meant to be so much more than that one controlling adjective.

SHE GLOWED

Every few weeks, Jade and I head out for a walk. It's nice being in her presence again. We chat about life and about the future. One overcast afternoon, we go for a walk and it begins to rain; she hands me her umbrella. "I love the rain," she assures me as she inhales the peaceful fresh-ness in the air.

I smile. I *know.*

"Did I ever tell you about what happened with Ana?" she asks me on one walk.

I look at her curiously, even though I've gradually become stoic towards Ana. What she said and did is in the past, and I won't let my memory of her haunt me.

"She told me she was into me, like romantically," Jade says.

Wow.

Ana ended up getting friend-zoned.

In that moment, though, the way Ana treated me made sense — it certainly didn't justify it, but it was at least an explanation. Deep down, Ana was hurt that Jade chose me over her. She'd been in love with Jade as well, all along; she'd been plagued with bitter jealousy. There's some relief in knowing that — sure, it's sad, but now I know more of why my childhood friend turned on me so suddenly and aggressively. Finally — closure.

As time passes, weeks build up between Jade and me hanging out.

The hands of a clock orbit its centre.

Texts become occasional. Rare.

White-throated sparrows perch on branches and fill the air with their whistles — haunting, peaceful.

The days get longer; the nights get shorter.

We slowly drift apart again.

In the depths of my mind, though, resides my last memory with her. We were walking through her neighbourhood. A bright, warm day —

Her green eyes survey the sky, sparkling in the sunlight. She raises her chin and closes her eyes.

THE NEW NORMAL

Lunch is much quieter without Olivia. I usually buy myself lunch, wander around 17th for a bit, then go back to the library to study. So many girls at school barely eat anything for lunch, and I would rather be alone than have my recovery sabotaged.

"You'll meet new people," Michelle tells me at a session. "Just give it time."

On Mondays, I start going to the GSA, a place full of new faces. Much to my relief, Ana never shows up (nor does Jade), and everyone there eats a reasonable amount.

There's a girl who's unusually thin, but I watch her force food down her throat. She takes a deep breath after eating and excuses herself to go for a walk. I barely know her, but I'm proud.

Everyone else there knows each other from the start of the year, and I can tell I'm on the outside of their circles, but they're still friendly. We make small talk, occasionally say hi when we pass in the hallways.

I make conversation with the people who sit around me in my classes, and offer help with schoolwork when they're confused. Every once in a while I'll go to Starbucks with one of them over lunch.

After school, I see the girls' volleyball team jaunt to the gymnasium for practice. They laugh and give each other high fives. I stand there as they pass, holding my books to my chest.

Maybe I'll join a sports team. That has to be a good way to meet people. *What would I do? Cross-country?*

Olivia and I text every day. She spends peaceful hours studying in the library — social studies is her favourite core course — and loses herself in painting and drawing projects in the art room. The people are friendly, and the community is welcoming.

She's happy.

I miss her.

When I take the bus, the earbud that would usually reside in Olivia's ear rests in my own.

MAGAZINES

I'm at the grocery store with Mom, waiting in the checkout line. Earlier this year, being in a grocery store would've brought me to tears, but I've come a long way.

I glance over at the magazine rack by the conveyor belt — three women's magazines promoting weight loss. One even boasts a way to "lose 11 pounds in a week." Before, that would've upset me. *Everyone wants to lose weight,* I would've thought. *Why are they allowed to, but I'm not?*

I know more now, though. All these magazines claiming to promote 'health' are ridiculous, but this promise to lose so much weight is especially absurd. As someone who's over-exercised, starved herself, and gotten herself dangerously thin, I can tell you — eleven pounds in a week is nearly impossible.

What a scam, I think, rolling my eyes.

My mom and I reach the front of the line, and I start unloading the contents of our cart. I lift up a cold carton of milk and lower it down on the conveyor belt.

Maybe part of the reason I'm so mad at these magazines is because I know why they're claiming all these unrealistic weight-loss strategies. They're trying to profit off people's insecurities. They don't give a shit about their reader's physical and mental health — the only thing they're worried about is profit.

There's a men's health magazine there, too. Unlike the women's magazines, the cover talks about endurance training, muscle exercises, and the wonders of the avocado.

Why does men's health equate to actual health, but women's health to weight loss?

The cashier scans the last of the groceries and puts the final one into a bag. "Thanks," my mom says. She turns to me and nods towards the door. "Let's roll."

I follow, leaving the magazines behind me.

As we walk through the parking lot, I can't stop thinking about how unethical some people will be to get you to buy their product. It's not just magazines, but clothing companies, too. The entire system. Flawed.

I've heard countless people say, "I want to lose weight" as a new year's resolution. I don't remember the last time I heard someone say, "I want to accept my body."

The further I get in my recovery, the more of the bigger picture I start to see.

So many people, always trying to shrink. And there's no end. *You can keep losing forever,* I'd like to tell them. *There is no end to Ed's losing game.*

This is what I know now: it's not your body that has to change; it's your mindset.

MY DEAREST PLAYER

Sometimes, I hear Ed's whispers echo through my mind.

'One day, Charlotte, I'll see you again. Maybe not next year; maybe not the year after that. Maybe not for a decade. But one day, we'll find each other. We always do. We might look a little different, but I'll recognize you, and you'll recognize me. One day, you'll let me out to play again.'

No, Ed, I say back. You cheated me at your own game. You promised me control and gave me anything but. You've given me chaos — turmoil, pain, fear. I quit your game.

I quit — for good.

eu·pho·ri·a

/yo͞oˈfôrēə/

noun

1. a feeling or state of intense excitement and happiness.

THE UNIVERSE

A hint of floral sweetness in the air.

Wet mud clumps around drainage gutters.

Pale clouds, tinged with gold wisps, float through the sky.

This evening, Olivia's coming over to my house for another sleepover. I text her:

> I have an idea.
>
> Come over on your bike
> and bring a swimsuit.

Later that day, Olivia pulls up to my garage on her bike, a backpack slung over her shoulder. She looks excited and curious.

"Are you gonna tell me what we're doing?" she asks.

"Soon," I say. I glance at the time on my phone. "We've just gotta wait until it gets a little darker. Come on in."

She nudges her kickstand down with her foot and we go inside to watch a movie as dusk falls. Eventually, my parents and Parker have all gone to bed, and the house is quiet.

When the movie finishes, she turns to me. "Okay, I can't handle the suspense anymore," she admits with a laugh. "What's the plan?"

"Put your swimsuit on and meet me in the garage in five," I announce.

She nods. I grab my swimsuit and run to the bathroom. Soon, we find ourselves standing in the garage.

"I think I know the perfect place to go night-swim-ming," I explain as I roll out my bike. "It's only a short bike ride away, at Sandy Beach."

"Ahh, I love this idea!" Olivia exclaims. "But we're not gonna get swept away, are we?"

"No, there's not much of a current."

We guide our bikes to the back alleyway; I close the garage door behind us.

"Follow me," I say.

And just like that, we're off. We coast through the dark streets, the moonlight coming from above show-ing us the way. I inhale the fresh night air. Warm wind ripples through my hair.

We bike through an empty dog park, until we get to a fence.

"We'll leave our bikes here," I say. "I brought a lock — we can lock them to this fence." I pause to secure the bikes.

Olivia runs her hand through the tall grass on our left, the strands weaving through her fingers.

There's a small opening in the fence, and a path that dives from the opening down into the brush below.

"Just down here, I think," I say. "I went past here on a walk with my family once."

"It's so dark," Olivia notes. "Do you want me to go first with the flashlight on my phone?"

"Yeah, good idea," I agree.

We edge down the path, stumbling over roots and large rocks. Branches brush against me on either side. The air is alive with the sound of crickets, the rushing of nearby water, and the shuffling of our feet.

Finally, we break out of the brush and to the riverside. I grin at our arrival. The ground drops steeply to make way for seven feet of water at a particular point. The water all around this deep area is relatively shallow. Olivia turns off her phone and puts it down on the ground. We walk up to the edge, and stand there for a moment: side by side, looking down at the remarkable clarity of the water.

Olivia glances over at me, and I glance over at her. We're both grinning.

"Let's do this!" she exclaims.

We slowly wade into the water through the shallow area. The water is cold, but not freezing; it ripples around our legs.

"It's chilly!" Olivia gasps.

"Only a bit!" I say. I push forwards into the deep area, completely submerging myself. I close my eyes as my head dunks underwater.

I don't shiver in the cool water. It feels as though it's my blood — carrying a steady stream of life throughout me.

There's no way I would've been able to do this last year — I would've frozen. But tonight, the water isn't painfully unpleasant — it's comfortably refreshing.

I once heard the universe gave this body to me as a rental, of sorts. I am not my body, and my body is not me; it's only a vessel for the real me. I'll use this body to go on great adventures and live life in, and then when the time comes, I'll leave it and go elsewhere. Eventually, it will be returned to the universe. It's my responsibility to take care of it in the meantime.

Olivia adjusts to the temperature quickly, and she swims out to the deep spot to join me.

We swim out into the darkness. The water is black, the trees are black, but the sky — it is alive, pulsating with distant planets, sparkling with stars, glowing with the moon.

For a while, we splash around. Then we float on our backs and stare up at the sky. The serene moon above us is full and clear — pearly white with splotches of silver.

I'm not going to tell you this world is perfect. I'm definitely not going to tell you it's easy. But there are some moments when time seems to freeze. In these moments, life comes easy, like a well-scripted movie we write as we go.

Maybe perfection comes in the moments we're not entirely in this world.

"This is beautiful," Olivia breathes.

We stay there, listening to the sounds of the night, basking in the pale moonlight.

Floating through the universe.

IT'S A STRANGE FEELING

Life doesn't move in linear motion.

Back when my mom took me to the emergency room — the time my blood pressure was at its record low — I worried it would feel like I was always trapped in that hospital room. I wasn't entirely wrong. Something strange happened, though. I'm still in the hospital room, yes — but I'm not trapped.

I don't know how to describe it, but it feels like I'm sitting at a hospital bedside, my younger version withering away — thin limbs beneath thin sheets.

I sit there with myself. I stare at this strange, dying girl.

I'm in control, witnessing and accepting how sick she is. She doesn't deserve this. I want to take away her pain, give her my strength. It feels so real.

Can you exist at multiple points in time at once?

DIFFICULT

Michelle and I discuss diet culture at our next session.

"Women who have been hurt by this system that determines beauty follow it religiously, despite it having such a negative impact on their lives," I say. "Isn't that a strange thing to do?"

"So why do you think they do it?" Michelle asks.

"Well, women pursue this set, so-called ideal — this mould — and encourage others to do the same," I say. "When the system that created the mould also created the pain that drives them to it."

Everything is starting to fit together. I see it now. "If the mould is the 'solution,' and poor body-image is the problem," I continue, "without the problem there would be no solution, but more importantly, *without the solution there would be no problem*. It's just people in positions of influence trying to capitalize off other, more vulnerable people, women in particular."

Michelle nods. "They create the problem to sell us the solution," she agrees. "So, what can we make of this whole system? What is its purpose for us?"

I stop and think about that. The only sound in the room is the soft ticking of a clock. Then, finally, I realize, "There isn't one." I look at her. "It's a losing game."

"There are two ways you can respond to the system. You can do what society wants you to do — be obedient. Or, you can be 'difficult,'" Michelle explains. "Which one do you want to be?"

It makes me think of a quotation from Naomi Wolf: *A cultural fixation on female thinness is not an obsession about female beauty but an obsession about female obedience.*

I say it in a heartbeat: "Difficult."

I WONDER WHAT IT ALL MEANS

When I wake up in the Deep, I crawl out of bed, wander through the house and out the door. The night air outside is calm, with a fresh, light breeze. The Mysterious Girl is standing motionless in the meadow, her back to me. Her hands rest at her sides, and her neck cranes to the sky. Grass sways around her shins. I walk up to her and stand at her side.

"The moon is so beautiful," she whispers.

I nod. It's true — it's a pale, glowing orb suspended in the darkness of the night sky, hanging among the stars.

She looks over at me. "Do you think you have it in you to fly again?"

"Yeah." I know I can do it; I trust myself now.

"Follow me, then."

She leads me back into the house and up the stairs. I climb out of the window after her, and we find ourselves standing on the roof, just like before.

"Jump with me, this time," the Mysterious Girl says.

Together, we sprint down the roof and jump out into the space before us. This time, though, we don't fall — from the moment our feet leave the roof, we're soaring upward.

She goes straight up — straight towards the moon — and I follow. She reaches out and touches it. Her fingers caress the white, bumpy surface. When she looks back, she must be able to see the shock on my face, because she says with a smile, "Like hope, things are never as far away as they seem."

I've got to stop being so surprised — this is the Deep, after all. Anything is possible. I reach out and touch the moon, too. It leaves a chalky dust on my fingertips.

The Mysterious Girl sits down on its cool surface, and I sit down beside her. It's much smaller than I would've expected — there's just enough space for the two of us.

Here it is — the Deep, all its shining stars and darkened alleyways, all its houses in neat little rows; all its glowing and peaceful streetlamps, warding off the darkness. It can get chaotic in the Deep, but when you really stop to look at it, it's stunning. "Whoa," I say, breathless. "The view from up here is beautiful."

"It's nice being able to see the big picture, isn't it," the Mysterious Girl responds.

This view really gets me thinking.

I've lived the past several months believing the only thing of importance for me was to be skinny. It's shocking, disturbing, even, what a sick mind will force you to believe.

I've gotten far enough in recovery to realize how wrong I was.

I ask the Mysterious Girl, "What is the purpose of life?" I've spent so long trapped in my own head I haven't looked at the world around me, and what it all means.

The eating disorder has been like locking myself in my house and boarding all the windows shut, refusing to go outside. The real world was a painful place, so I would hide from it. Now, though, I'm unlocking doors, taking down the boards, opening the windows. I'm learning there's a world beyond all this, one with so much to explore and learn from.

Now is a time for rediscovery, of sorts.

"You're in no rush to figure anything out — you've got your whole life ahead of you," the Mysterious Girl answers.

"I know," I agree. "I do like to think about it, though."

She looks off into the distance, lost in thought. "One day, the sun will sputter out and die," she says.

In the sky, a distant star blinks.

Disappears.

Darkness fills where it was.

"Astronomers are guessing the sun has anywhere between seven to eight billion years left before it eventually burns out. It's a long time, but it's far from forever. The heat will take all life from earth, turning it into a lifeless rock floating through space. Everything we know to exist in our lives will be gone, just like that — our existence is temporary."

I think back to earlier this year, and all the time I spent in hospitals. As I lay amongst the hissing of blood-pressure cuffs and the beeping of heart monitors, I understood that my existence is temporary. I became so well acquainted with my mortality — after everything, I always will be.

"Everything is both temporary and purposeful, even if it isn't easily noticeable at a first glance," she continues. "Whatever the purpose of life is, it's not permanence."

I agree with her.

"The rest, though, is up to you to figure out," she says.

She puts her head on my shoulder, and we watch the

Deep throughout the night. The breeze gently sweeps through the streets, around the moon, and through my hair.

All I know is I want to be authentic.

Just imagine all the power you could unlock simply by being yourself.

Maybe our purpose is to leave an impact on those around us, the long-lasting influence of emotion.

Feelings — mementos of the past, living on inside us — carefully preserved in glass frames of memory.

The mind — a museum for beaming smiles, wet eyes, flushed skin. The halls go on infinitely.

One day, we'll be gone. But if we've really made someone feel something, are we really?

"I'm going to keep searching for a purpose," I promise.

The Mysterious Girl smiles. "I think you owe that to yourself."

HOME

My *body feels* a little more like home every day.

FLORA

I *missed half of my* Grade 10 English classes to go to therapy. My teacher was filled in on the entire situation and was very supportive throughout it all. In Grade 11, I would be lucky enough to get to have her again. She would walk up to me on the first day of classes and look at me. "I'm back," I'd say with a smile. Without words, she would hug me.

When Parker looks over at me with his eager eyes; when Olivia explodes with laughter; hugs, firm and secure, when the curve of a torso and the bend of an elbow fit together like puzzle pieces . . . I see something beyond this world — the faintest trace of something with the power to live forever.

Often, I hear people say, "Everything happens for a reason." Then why do horrible things happen to innocent people? Why do we go through pain with no real benefit? I wouldn't say everything happens for a reason, but as my mom says, "Everything that happens brings us somewhere important."

Sometimes, I wonder if I'll ever be the same as I was prior to my illness. But I don't think recovery is about getting back to where you were before. It's about creating something new. It's a demonstration of your strength — it's your chance to redefine who you are and what you stand for.

Humans grow like plants, and life blossoms like flowers. Sometimes you don't realize a flower's fullest beauty because it hasn't bloomed yet. All the beauty is there, though, carefully hidden in the folds of leaves surrounding the bud. Sometimes you just have to patiently wait for it to open up to the sun.

FRESH STARTS

I *stare into* the bathroom mirror.

"Oh my god," I whisper, my eyes wide with horror.

My mom walks up behind me and puts her hand on my shoulder. "It's definitely time for a haircut," she says.

I've really let my hair go. My pixie cut has turned into an unkempt mullet, and my roots are two inches long. The hair that was once dyed icy blonde is now a bronzing yellow. It's a tragedy, really. *How did I not notice this sooner?*

But at least it's grown back. No more balding for me.

I don't want to look the way I did before, though. I want things to be different this time — I feel different, after all. It's a new me.

"What are we thinking today?" my hairdresser asks me at the salon.

I look at myself in the mirror for a moment. "Dye it black," I request.

My hairdresser looks surprised. I've been dying my hair blonde for over two years now. "Are you sure?" she asks.

I nod, not taking my eyes off myself. I need this change.

A couple hours later, I walk out with my hair trimmed and jet black.

"Wow," my dad says, looking just as surprised as the hairdresser did when I mentioned black.

"I like it," Parker chimes in.

"It makes your eyes pop," my mom notes.

I love it.

Several nights later, I wake up in the Deep. My window is open; the night air is calm and warm. I head to the window. No one in the field tonight.

I head downstairs and pass a nearly finished puzzle sitting on the dining room table. I don't remember that being there before. Despite the churning colours of the pieces, when they fit together, something new and unexpected is formed. Darkness and light. "It's beautiful," I whisper.

Taking my time, I wander through the village, noticing and appreciating every detail I stumble across. The streets are quiet this evening. I turn a corner and see a woman holding hands with a younger girl — her daughter, I assume. They're both smiling, and their clasped hands swing as they walk.

I don't see anyone else on my walk, but I don't mind. I don't feel lonely — the solitude is peaceful. I loop back around to begin returning in the direction of my house, when I find a mirror standing in the middle of the road. The bottom is brushed with dust and dirt from the street, but the top is remarkably clean.

I stare at it as I approach, and I see the Mysterious Girl walking up to me. When I reach the mirror, we stare at each other. I smile. She smiles back.

I feel a swell of pride. "It really was you," I say to my reflection. "It was you, all along."

EVERYTHING

It's a cool spring evening, and my room is filled with fresh air as I sit by my window, my phone in hand. I look out at the world moving by outside. The sky glows with twilight, and lights inside houses glow warmly against the approaching dark. The streetlights are just starting to turn on.

I text Olivia:

> What's your definition of beautiful?

I realize how skewed my view of beauty has been for so long, how society has tainted and altered it to fit inside its conventional mould. Society definitely has a definition, but I don't know if there really is one. Olivia answers quickly.

Oh wow big question

I see the three dots floating on her side of the screen; I patiently wait. Then she says exactly what I've been starting to realize.

I think we are all made to be the way we were meant to be, and who we are is who we are. We should parade that, accept that, and the world should accept that, too. The world is beautiful, and we are all beautiful. The world moves in a beautiful circle.

Everything it grows and makes, everything
that lives, is beautiful. And so there really
is no definition of beautiful.

I agree

And for the first time, I really believe it.
How can we try to squish something into a mould of
'beauty' when beauty is in everything?

I THINK THAT'S BEAUTIFUL

Tornados have four stages: storm development, storm organization, tornado formation, and tornado dissipation. I think I've finally made it to the last stage; I think this storm is finally over.

I sit down on my bed with a pencil and notebook in my lap, and I think about everything I've gone through this past year. In the end, it's left me with a strange, complicated feeling. Maybe it's simply the feeling of being alive.

What *does* it feel like to be alive?

Withdrawal, dysphoria, euphoria.
Noise in the silence, silence in the noise.
A raw aching that leaks from your chest to the rest of your body like ink in water.
Motion — falling first, then flying.

A small smile tugs at the corners of my mouth. I realize how grateful I am to be here.

I think about all the other people who have felt their own variations of the feeling of being alive, and what a special thing it is. I wish there was some way to capture it, and share the wonders of it with all the people who haven't fully come to understand it yet; I just wish there was a way I could give someone a glimmer of hope about this delicate, complex, imperfect thing. Life.

Maybe there is.

I stare at the blank page below me for a moment. And I begin to write.

Over the course of the next several months, I get further and further along — my whole experience, taking form on paper. I work on it diligently — whether I'm feeling crushed or elated, I channel it in. The project grows throughout my recovery. I'm not sure what's going to become of this book. Maybe it will help other people who find themselves stuck in my situation. Maybe it will remain an unpolished draft stored away in a folder on my bookshelf, a personal testament to what I was able to overcome. Either way, I'm happy.

Here it is.

This is it.

I wander through the streets by my house, late in the evening. The sky, glowing with the final traces of twilight — until night arrives. Streetlamps flick on, orbs of warm light that fade out into darkness. The delicate singing of birds, echoing from distant trees. The gentle rush of cars passing by the outskirts of the neighbourhood.

I close my eyes; inhale. The night air is fresh and dewy, with a quiet whisper of firepit smoke. *I'm the only thing that will ever come at all close to being me.*

Inside the houses, people mill about — twenty-somethings with flushed faces clinking glasses of wine and laughing with vigour. Families nestled together in blankets as they watch movies. An elderly woman, lines etched in her face, drinking a lonely cup of tea at the kitchen counter. Each with their own troubles and dreams.

All of them, vessels of things that exist solely in their memory.

Messy; flawed; beautiful.

I arrive at my childhood park. My feet crunch against the pebbles, and I sit down on one of the swings.

Rest my hands on the cool chains.

Look up.

I never realized how much of an impact light pollution has until now. You just can't see much from the city. I squint up at the little blinking satellites and pretend they're stars.

ACKNOWLEDGEMENTS

First, I'd like to thank Juno House for teaching me critical thinking and how to be the strongest version of myself possible. So much of my wisdom, I gained from you. You were right when you said no one leaves Juno without becoming a feminist.

A special thank you to Rosemary Nixon, Kelsey Attard, and Naomi K. Lewis for helping me polish and share my story. Women in literature! Hurrah!

I'm beyond grateful for Ms. Cameron, who was my English teacher throughout all of high school, as well as my mentor and supporter from day one. Thank you for always checking in on me after class in Grade 10, back during the most difficult stage of my recovery, and for wholeheartedly listening to all my excited book updates in Grades 11 and 12. Your encouragement meant so, so much.

This book is my interpretation of lived experiences. Some scenes and characters are composites of the actual events and people. Names of people have been changed to protect their identities.

Charlotte Bellows wrote *The Definition of Beautiful*, her debut book, while attending high school. She grew up in Calgary, Alberta, and has left to live her most beautiful life. She may be back.

~~teenage~~

~~intimate~~

Bellows's ^account of her struggle
with anorexia reads like a diary:
intimate and sometimes ~~deep honestly~~ openly
&awkward,
despairing. It's a remarkably candid
story, ~~so much so that~~ a remarkable
achievement for a writer so young.

~~Her path is a narrow one~~

When I compare her account with
those of Andrews + Clarren, ~~I can~~
~~see that~~ with their admirable
awareness of the perilous issues
of our time (global warming, erasure
pitiless attacks on Indigenous ~~people~~,
gun violence, antisemitisms),
            self-obsessive!
Bellows' ^path is a narrower one.
But a brave one. She's a writer to
watch. ~~In the D's... beautiful, there is~~
~~there~~ there is, of necessity, a great
~~deal of self-obsessive detail~~